SEA MUSIC

SEA MUSIC

Christina Green

CHIVERS

British Library Cataloguing in Publication Data available

This Large Print edition published by AudioGO Ltd, Bath, 2012.
Published by arrangement with the Author

U.K. Hardcover   ISBN   978 1 4458 2733 9
U.K. Softcover   ISBN   978 1 4458 2734 6

Printed and bound in Great Britain by
MPG Books Group Limited

A BID FOR FREEDOM

'Miss Charlotte, please keep still—I'm afraid One of these pins will stick in you if you keep twisting around like that.'

Charlotte Westland looked down at the woman pinning up the hem of the new ballgown, and sighed. 'I'm sorry, Mrs Albert, it's just that . . .' She stopped, her gaze turning to the window and the view stretching from it.

The sea in all its glory, calm today and not running the white horses of waves that she loved so much. In her mind she heard the soft, lilting music of the water as it flowed towards the shore, and somewhere out there, Andy and his little boat. She wished, with all her heart, that she could throw off the flounces and yards of muslin and taffeta, tell poor Mrs Albert to throw away the pins and go home, because she didn't want to wear the new gown. She wanted to be out there, in the boat, with Andy.

But, of course, Aunt Jemima had the last word. 'Charlotte, it's most important that you look your best at the midsummer county ball. Next month, you'll be seventeen, child, and it's high time that you found a husband. And no-one will bother to look at you if you're not dressed well. So kindly allow Mrs Albert to finish fitting the gown.'

Another sigh, but Aunt Jem was not to be

1

argued with. 'I'm sorry, Mrs Albert. I really will try and stand still.'

The fitting continued and Mrs Albert ventured a compliment or two as she knelt beside Charlotte and finished pinning up the scalloped hem.

'How well this pale blue muslin suits you, Miss Charlotte. Goes so well with your peachy complexion and your bright eyes. And when you've had your hair dressed and something pretty around your neck, you'll be the belle of the ball, I'm sure of it.'

'She will be wearing the pretty string of pearls that were handed down to me by my dear mother, and which will now be hers.' Aunt Jem's smile was wide and she nodded at Charlotte, as if to assure her that what Mrs Albert said would come true.

The belle of the ball? Not if I can help it, thought Charlotte. She had other, far more important things to think about than smiling at strange and inarticulate young men in an overheated ballroom and allowing them to tread on her toes because, of course, none of them would know how to dance properly.

Another sigh. Oh, to be out there, in the salty air, with the gulls shrieking as she and Andy Reddaway, her childhood friend and ally, brought the boat home over the bar and off-loaded their catch. But once this fitting was over and Aunt Jem had stopped planning the arrangements for the summer ball, she could escape.

It was not until luncheon was finished that she found the chance to slip outside, saying, as usual, with her fingers crossed behind her back—well, it was only half a lie, after all—that she was going to the beach to collect shells from the newly ebbing tide. She must keep up with her hobby of shell craft work. Aunt Jem approved of this, so there were no arguments about leaving the house, although Papa eyed her with an expression that made her wonder just what he was thinking. He knew most of her tricks, but then, he treated her like the son he had never had, so what did he expect? Actually calling her Charlie said it all.

So she went quickly through the garden and then, avoiding Eddie, the groom's, eye she ran past the stables, down the lane and on towards the beach. Andy Reddaway would be there, she knew it; his boat, the *Daisy Ann* would be beached above the tideline and he would be busily making sure that everything was secure and ready for the next excursion.

Wending her way along the cliff path, Charlie soon turned off down the steep, rough track leading to the beach below. The big cave known as the Devil's Whisper because of the echo of the waves filling it at high tide, was a favourite hiding place and now she followed the usual procedure.

Slipping down into its dark depths, she found the small ledge high behind some dry rocks and the old tin trunk where she always stored her Charlotte clothes when about to become Charlie, embarking on a sea-going adventure with Andy.

Take off the dress and shawl, crumple up the ridiculous petticoats, put on the old pair of Andy's breeches that were almost too small for her now, change her kid slippers for rough boots, slip into the oversized linen shirt that she had filched from Papa's cupboard when he wasn't looking, put her own clothes into the trunk and close the lid, and there—she was ready for the next exciting part of the afternoon.

Suitably dressed, tying her long hair behind her head, Charlie strode down the beach and presented herself to Andy, who looked up, and nodded.

'I'm ready. Where are we going?' she asked. 'I couldn't get away earlier, Aunt Jem was going on about this wretched ball I have to attend soon and then Papa wanted to talk to me about meeting a suitable young man. He wants me to marry very soon. It's all so boring.'

She sat on the gunwhale of the boat and sniffed the air, delighting in the familiar scents of salt and fish. 'Balls are so stuffy and everybody wears flowers that smell overpowering. I wish I could get out of going.'

Andy put down his hammer and looked at her and she saw something in his direct, tawny-eyed gaze that was upsetting. Even his voice

4

sounded different.

He cleared his throat before saying slowly, and looking away from her, 'But you can't pretend to be a boy much longer, I mean, you don't look like one any longer, Charlie. Your papa's right, you're growing up. Soon you'll marry and have to get used to being a wife.' He stopped, swallowed loudly. 'And you'll have a family, too ...'

Had he said too much? He looked away, pretending not to notice the colour racing into her cheeks as his meaning began to make sense. Distressing sense and, of course, he was right, Charlie thought grudgingly. She probably couldn't expect to have adventures for much longer.

Her natural defiance rushed in and words erupted. 'I won't! I'll run away to sea rather than do that! Women are so boring, so ordinary, they never do anything exciting ...'

Just recently, they had had this argument every time that Charlie was able to slip away from the house and sail off with him, but never quite in such a serious tone as today. All she wanted was to launch the *Daisy Ann* and sail out to collect Andy's crab pots, and then back into one of the nearby little bays, where they would fish, bringing back baskets of their catch which Andy sold in the village, while she carried her bag of shells back to Headland House. But today was different, and he didn't seem to want to go.

5

Now he sat next to her and, avoiding her eyes, looked at the horizon. 'And another thing, Charlie. There's talk of more smuggling,' he said carefully. 'A lugger was seen last night, hovering around the headland. I don't think we should go out today. It's not safe if they're planning a landing tonight.'

Charlie's eyes widened and she stared at him. 'Smuggling? But we know it goes on all the time, nobody really minds. Why, even Aunt Jem has some lace and silks that came from goodness knows where, and as for Papa, where does he get all the brandy he likes so much? Don't be silly, Andy, there's no danger at all.'

She got up, traced her name in the sand beside the boat with the toe of her boot, and then looked at him again, smiling, trying to make him change his mind. 'I'm not afraid of smugglers, Andy Reddaway, even if you are.'

He stood up, looking at her with a very straight face and a frown on his suntanned face.

'Say what you like, Charlie. I'm not taking you out in the *Daisy Ann* today. Of course we know about bits of smuggling here and there, it's part of village life, but from all I hear, this one is more than that. It could be a really big job; there's talk of men being armed, and it's a boat we've never seen before. All that and the revenue men are about. You must go home. Yes, you must.'

'I shan't!' Disappointment filled her voice,

6

but it was the other things he had said that really made her behave so childishly. About growing up. Marrying . . .

He shrugged, picked up his bag and jacket from inside the boat, and turned towards the village. 'Sorry, Charlie, but we're not going. So go home and keep safe.' He started walking up the beach.

Charlie stood quite still, staring after him. She couldn't believe all that he had said. Never mind about growing up—her thoughts flew to smuggling. But no-one bothered about smuggling, it went on all the time. Could it be—she frowned—that Andy was afraid? Surely not. They had had small adventures over the years when they had sailed out together since early childhood and he had always been so brave. But now—even Andy was taking care not to get involved in what this strange boat might be up to.

Charlie sat on the side of the *Daisy Ann* again, watching him as he plodded up the beach, finally disappearing from sight, and found herself thinking more sensibly than usual.

Was it possible that, as Andy had said, she must stop pretending to be a boy and grow up into a proper young woman? Did balls and marriage contracts really loom ahead of her? And had Papa finally set his mind to treating her like a daughter, rather than the son he had hoped for? Must Charlie, with tied back hair and tight breeches, now become Charlotte in the flouncy new ballgown, and wear the family pearls around her throat?

She gave a last long, yearning look out to sea. Yes, Andy was right. There was a big lugger anchored not far off shore. Hovering, the villagers called it, waiting for the tide to be right and the moon no longer as bright as it had been over the last few nights. Smugglers, men armed, rowing into the bay on their little boats, off-loading their contraband on to the carts and barrows that certain villagers would have waiting for them. A shiver of excitement ran down her spine.

How wonderful it would be if she, Charlie again, could be there, to watch it all going on. Was it possible that, if she really had to give up sailing with Andy, she could manage to slip out of the house tonight on a final adventure?

But then the passionate feeling died, and she walked slowly back to the cave, climbed up to the hiding hole, and changed her clothes, leaving the old breeches and boots and shirt there in the trunk where no-one would ever find them, and then traced her steps back to the house. She felt as if something big had happened in her life; the carefree days with Andy in the *Daisy Ann* were over, and her future waited for her.

Reaching the house, she went slowly up to her bedroom and sat down by the window, reaching for her journal. 'Today,' she wrote wretchedly, 'my life is changing'. Then she went down to the drawing-room for tea with Papa and Aunt Jem, and wondered whether this was the time to tell them about the strange lugger in the bay. Or was it just possible that they already knew and were making arrangements to accept the contraband brought in?

Aunt Jem was already pouring tea, when Charlotte came into the drawing-room. 'We were wondering where you were, Charlotte. As you can see, Jane has come to take tea with us. So nice to see her.' She paused, teapot in hand. 'Milk and sugar, my dear?'

Jane Edwards, the local doctor's daughter and Charlie's closest friend, smiled politely. 'Thank you, Miss Westland. Very little milk and no sugar, thank you.' She looked across the room at Charlotte, seating herself within the circle around the fireplace. 'I've brought you news of next week's church bazaar, Charlie. Mrs Endacott, the organiser, would like you to take some of your shell work for her craft stall. Shall we go together?'

Aunt Jem tutted. 'I should be glad if you would no longer use that tomboyish name, Jane. Her papa and I think it high time that Charlotte answered to her true name.' She allowed herself a smile. 'So pretty and feminine. Well, Charlotte, I'm sure you will like to go with Jane?'

Charlie smiled at Jane and knew they were

9

thinking the same thing, that Aunt Jem loved laying down the law, but that somehow they would manage to get round her. Then she thought more deeply. Was Aunt Jem right? Should she be more like Jane, who was always tidy, soft voiced and well dressed? And Jane always said the right things, too. A bit dull perhaps, but a good friend for all that. And what was she on about now—a bazaar? Not so exciting as thinking of an adventure to watch the smugglers bringing their cargo ashore.

But Aunt Jem was frowning again, clearly expecting a proper answer, so she accepted a slice of seed cake and said carefully, 'What a good idea, Jane. When we've had tea I'll show you the latest arrangement of shells I've made.'

She managed to wink at her friend, who raised one eyebrow and applied herself to her teacup. Then Papa came in late and more tea had to be ordered, but they sat around talking about the bazaar while he drank two cups and finished off the seed cake,

Then Charlie rose, looking at Jane with a definite purpose in her smile. 'Shall we go up to my room?' she asked, and with a nod from Aunt Jem, led Jane out into the hallway.

Going up the staircase, she whispered, 'So much to tell you, Jane. I thought we'd never get away from Papa and Aunt Jem.'

Jane asked, 'But why did you have to get away? Is it a secret, what you have to tell me?'

10

Charlie opened the door of her room, and went straight away to her table beneath the window where her shell work lay, while Jane sat neatly on the bed.

Charlie turned and looked at her, and then, trying to keep the excitement from her voice, she said quickly, 'Yes, it's a secret, and one that I can only tell to you, Jane, so listen to this. I'm going to sneak out of the house tonight and watch the men from the boat in the bay bring ashore their contraband.'

Jane flinched. 'You mean—smugglers? Oh, Charlie, it sounds quite awful. I mean, smugglers are really bad men—they could harm you, or even kidnap you . . .' Her pale eyes were wide, her face fixed in an expression of horror. Charlie could have laughed, if the last word hadn't set her pulses racing.

'Kidnap me?' she breathed. 'I hadn't thought of that. Oh, but what an adventure that would be.'

'Please don't do anything silly,' pleaded Jane, clasping her hands together.

But Charlie was at the window, staring out into the gathering dusk, making plans. A couple of hours before it was really dark, and then she would go.

ACTING LIKE A LADY

Would it never get dark? Charlie watched the moon slipping between rapidly flowing grey clouds and waited impatiently for the complete blackness that she knew would allow the smugglers to off-load their goods and start the journey to places of storage. But at times the moonlight was almost too bright for the purpose. She sat by her window, shawl wrapped around her shoulders, waiting, waiting . . .

Downstairs she heard voices in the study. Papa and his friend Mr Harvey Jackson drinking brandy, no doubt, and enjoying their talk. But at last Mr Jackson's voice sounded louder and she knew they were in the hall, Papa seeing Mr Jackson on his way back to his own house, further down the village.

Soon, she thought, the house would be properly silent. And the moon must soon move around so that its light wasn't so annoying— and then she heard a knock at her door.

'May I come in, Charlotte? You're up very late. Is anything the matter?'

She tensed. Papa must have seen the glimmer of candlelight beneath the door. What did he want? And he would wonder why she was not in bed. Quickly she flew away from the window, pulling on a wrapper to try and hide the fact that she was still dressed. 'Just a moment, Papa,' she called, but he was already opening the door, looking at her with a frown on his face.

'Since you are still awake, I want to take the opportunity to talk to you very seriously, my dear daughter. Shall we sit down?'

Charlotte nodded and sat on her bed, watching while he folded himself into the chair by the window. 'Now, you must realise that what I have to say is for your own good, Charlie.' He frowned, and then smiled apologetically. 'I mean, Charlotte, of course.' He looked at her and Charlie thought he looked a little sad. However, he went on determinedly. 'Mr Jackson, Harvey, has just left. We had matters to discuss after dinner and he has told me about village gossip, which I find most distressing. And it concerns you, my dear girl.'

Charlie tensed. Had he found out about her changing her clothes and sailing off with Andy? But she had imagined Papa must have known she did that, though he had never said anything, even if he did. Aunt Jem never knew, of course; imagine her horror if she had known! Charlie stifled a grin.

Papa was going on, his face sterner now, his voice firmer. 'Perhaps I have been too lenient over the years, Charlotte. The fact that you have always been inclined to be a bit of a tomboy has often made me think of you almost

13

as a son.

'So your little escapades with young Andy Reddaway seemed to be innocent. When you were both children, and he came into the garden while his father was working here, it seemed natural for you to play together. But now someone in the village has spread the gossip that you have been seen going sailing with the lad, and actually wearing men's clothing, and this I certainly cannot dismiss.' He looked at her very solemnly and Charlie felt colour rushing into her cheeks. 'What have you to say, Charlotte?'

'Well . . .' She thought hard, but there was no way out, the truth must be acknowledged. As a magistrate, Papa was always fair, although he was a true disciplinarian. She felt sure he wouldn't punish her too badly if she confessed. 'Yes, Papa, I do put on breeches and a shirt—an old one of yours, actually,' she saw his expression lift—was it a brief smile—and went on rapidly, 'and boots, because slippers are useless in a boat . . .' Anxiously watching him, she thought she saw a hint of amusement lighten his dark eyes, quickly concealed as he cleared his throat and looked down at the floor. Then he was his usual strict self again.

'Thank you for being truthful, dear girl. And, even although I am deeply shocked that you should resort to such extreme behaviour, I do understand that my treatment of you

14

is probably as much to blame as your own waywardness. So we will forget the whole business—except of course, you must realise that these trips out with young Reddaway must instantly stop.' He looked at her more kindly and Charlotte bowed her head, trying to accept all that he said.

But her mind was whirling, and she could hardly believe that her life had to change so desperately, and so quickly. No more sailing, no more collecting crab pots and fishing, no more having fun with Andy . . . then she looked up as Papa went on speaking and realised that there was still worse to come.

'So, Charlotte, in view of all these disobedient secrets you have hidden from us, you must now try to act in the way a girl of your status and upbringing should, and that means we must find a husband for you. You need to marry and settle down—somewhere, I hope, not too far away—but in a pleasant house where you can raise a family and live happily with your husband for the remainder of your life.'

He was smiling at her, the familiar loving Papa whose thoughts were always of what was right for his only child. And he was waiting for her to reply—to say 'yes' to all of it, to do as he asked. To change her life . . .

Charlie heard her voice grow unsteady as she finally found words to reply. Indeed, she was almost trembling, as she said slowly, 'I shall find it very hard, Papa, to stop seeing my friend, Andy, and going out in his boat; but I do understand that it is too shocking for the village to know that I actually wear men's clothing . . . and I will stop doing so. As for marriage . . .' she could not go on.

Papa was telling her exactly what Andy had said, and to have such advice from the two people who were her greatest friends was dreadful. But she supposed there was no way out. 'Yes, Papa, I must marry, and soon. I know that being seventeen is the right age to find a husband '

'That's my dear, good daughter.' He leaned across the space and put a hand on her shoulder. She met his smiling eyes and bravely blinked away her own tears. 'And when you attend the summer ball very soon, I am quite sure there will be several young men who will see how lovely you are, and then come to me with requests to tell you of their admiration. And then you can make your choice . . .'

The ball. The new dress. The single rope of pearls. The overpowering smell of flowers and her toes being trodden on . . . Charlie hung her head and screwed up her eyes. Somewhere she had to find the courage to accept all that now was fated to come her way. But, even if she was shocked at what lay ahead, she had always been brave, so she met her father's eyes and nodded to him.

'Very well, Papa. I will try to do exactly what

16

you ask of me.' A happy thought flew into her racing mind. Perhaps no young man would approach her? Perhaps she could go on being Charlie for a little longer? Words flew into her mouth. 'I mean, when the time comes.'

Her Papa looked at her with suspicious eyes, but simply said, 'Very well. And now it's past our bedtime, so sleep well, dear daughter, and I hope your dreams will be of the good life that waits for you.' He rose, and went towards the door, where he looked back at her and smiled. 'Remember, Charlotte could well be even more exciting than Charlie . . .' and then left the room.

Charlie, must she really think of herself as Charlotte, sat where she was, listening to his footsteps fading, and his door finally closing behind him before she got up and went to the window. She stared out. The moon was slipping in and out of the dark clouds, and a breeze had risen, soughing through the trees at the back of the house. Suddenly her eyes widened.

Was it horses' hooves she heard, clip-clopping nearer, now entering the cliff path that wound so close to the front of the house as it journeyed on towards the next bay? Forgetting everything else, she twisted back the curtain, opened the window and leaned out, peering into the darkness. Yes, there were moving shapes there—even darker shadows, ponies laden with packages, sounds of bodies shifting on their saddles, the jingles of bridles —and then the moon slipped into a wide space of cloudless sky and beamed down.

A troop of horsemen was passing beneath her window. Charlie cried, 'Oh!' and then put a hand to her mouth, but too late, the last rider in the line had heard, was pulling at his reins and looking up towards her window.

The moonlight shone on his face and she had a clear view of a young man with shadowed but chiseled features, wearing a hat that didn't quite cover his curling hair; his eyes seemed to gleam beneath the pale light, and he was looking at her. He smiled, raised a hand as if in salute, and then continued on his way, following his companions, down the path, into the darkness of the night.

Charlie sank into the chair Papa had just vacated, her mind wheeling and her blood singing. Smugglers, of course—but who was he, that handsome, strong looking man who had smiled with such laughter in his eyes? Where was he going? And then the strangest, most disturbing feeling of all—would she ever see him again?

Next day she sought to forget the excitement of last night. After Papa's startling edict her dreams had been unsettled—an image of Andy's little boat bobbing on enormous waves, and then another of someone else—a man on horseback, whose bright eyes were still in her mind when she awoke.

18

But, with a sigh, Charlie recalled her duty, and paid extra attention to her toilette before going down to breakfast. If she was going to discuss the church bazaar arrangements with Jane and Mrs Endacott, she would try and look a proper young lady.

Aunt Jem's critical eyes noticed the difference at once. She smiled approvingly as Charlie sat down. 'You look very well, this morning, Charlotte. Your hair seems to know its place much better than usual . . .'

Charlie couldn't help a blush, and saw Papa concealing a smile as he added his own approval. 'Such a pretty dress, too—I don't recall seeing it for some time. It suits you well, my dear.'

Charlie ate her breakfast sedately and tried to focus her whirling thoughts. Bazaar. Shell work. Jane—and no more memories of the troop of smugglers who had passed beneath her window last night.

It was hard work, but by the time the meal was over, she was ready to return to her room and collect the latest piece of finished shell work which she intended to produce for Mrs Endacott's approval. And Jane would be here very soon. As she tied her bonnet and went downstairs she heard the knock at the door and ran to open it.

'I'm ready, Jane. Shall we walk down or would you care to have a cup of chocolate first?' Manners, thought Charlie, pleased with herself She supposed she must cultivate good manners if she was to make Papa proud of her, but Jane was eager to get on.

'No, thank you. I am to accompany Mama on some social calls this afternoon, so mustn't be late for luncheon.' Her pale eyes sparkled. 'Oh, Charlie, have you heard about the new gentleman who, with his sister, has bought The Look Out, the old house on the cliff? Well, we're going there to call on them, isn't it exciting?'

'Is it?' Charlie picked up her shell work bag and followed her friend down the path. She wasn't much interested in new neighbours but of course, Jane, being a model young lady, loved all the social chitchat that went on when new people moved into the village.

Jane, carrying her small portfolio of paintings under her arm as they walked briskly along, glanced at Charlie with an exasperated expression. 'Really, Charlie, will you never learn? We have to meet new people— especially if we are of marriageable age, like you and me. Perhaps this new young man will be handsome, and rich, and . . .' By now she was smiling blissfully and Charlie couldn't resist bringing her back to earth.

'And probably already engaged to someone else. Wake up, Jane!'

'Oh, Charlie! How can you be so horrible? I was just dreaming, really, because it's important I meet someone soon. After all, I'm a year older than you, so I'm really getting on.' Jane's pretty face fell and Charlie was soon apologising.

'Sorry, Jane. I was only teasing. Yes, perhaps this new man will be ready to fall at your feet—so make sure you wear your prettiest gown this afternoon. Well, here we are at Mrs Endacott's, so let's see what she thinks of our craft work, shall we?'

*   *   *

Mrs Endacott's welcome was warm, her lined face one big smile. She led them into the farmhouse kitchen and put a plate of warm, freshly buttered scones on the table and poured milk into two glasses. 'Some refreshments while we talk, young ladies?' She gestured them to sit at two chairs opposite her and then sank heavily into her own, creaking cane chair beside the fire. 'Now let me see what you have brought with you. Miss Charlotte, I hope it's one of your lovely shell flowers?'

Charlie untied her bag and set the flower arrangement on the table. 'I've just finished it, Mrs Endacott. If it sells then I can always make another one.'

They looked at the shining blossoms formed by the shells that were fixed together with wire. Mrs Endacott said, 'Why, it's just lovely, Miss Charlotte! What a lot of different shells.

Where do you find them?'

'In the bay, mostly. But sometimes Papa's friends who come home from abroad bring me really exotic shells.'

Charlie was glowing with pleasure, for her craft work meant much to her. She loved creating flowers from the unlikely shapes of turret shells, periwinkles of all sizes and colours, and long, sharp razor shells; the common blue of the scoop-shaped mussel, and even the strange, fanciful Pelican's foot, not often found. Limpets, winkles, clams and whelks—all found when walking the tide line on the beach—such a hotchpotch of colours and shapes. And there, in the centre of the arrangement, reflecting the sunlight and shining out a like a precious jewel among the humbler shells, a piece of Mother of Pearl.

For a moment her mind flashed to Aunt Jem's words, about Mother's string of pearls to be worn at the ball, and she wondered if real pearls were to be found on the beach, but then she was back in the farmhouse, and Mrs Endacott was inviting her to try another scone while, in turn, Jane opened her portfolio and showed her new painting of the sea on a wild day. High, white-tipped waves, and green frightening depths. Charlie thought that, for an ordinary girl like Jane, the picture was extremely good, and full of the mystery of the ocean.

And that brought another mystery into her

mind. The smuggler last night looking up at her and smiling . . .

VISITING NEW NEIGHBOURS

The days passed very slowly now that Charlie was unable to slip out of the house and find Andy. She spent some time working at her shell flowers, having left the arrangement for sale with Mrs Endacott, and now found her stock of shells was running low.

Her aunt removed her spectacles, looked at her very thoughtfully and, after a short silence, nodded her head. 'Very well, Charlotte. But don't be too long. And don't even think of going anywhere else . . .' Her eyes were knowledgeable, and Charlie understood that she really must resist all ideas of adventures.

'Thank you, Aunt. And, no, of course, I won't leave the bay. I'll be back in good time for luncheon.'

'Yes, make sure you are. I would like you to accompany me this afternoon. Some new people, the Reeds, have moved into The Look Out and we must call on them.'

Charlie's mood lightened. She smiled. 'Yes, Jane was telling me about them yesterday. A young man and his sister, I believe. How nice to have new neighbours.'

Aunt Jem's voice was flat. 'We shall see.

23,

Well, run along, dear child, and don't get your feet wet.'

Charlie left the room, fuming. *Don't get your feet wet, indeed!* Oh, how she would love to do just that, taking off stockings and slippers and kicking rapturously through the lacy waves as they spilled onto the beach.

The bay was deserted. No *Daisy Ann* there—of course, thought Charlie unhappily. Andy would be out fishing and seeing to his crab pots. But somehow she forced away the sad thoughts and walked along the tide line, searching for the shells which would enable her to continue with her craft work.

And then suddenly, there was a call. 'Charlie! Hello!'

She stared around. No-one. Then she looked up at the cliff top, and there was Jane sitting at her easel, waving and smiling. It took Charlie only a few minutes to climb along her own personal path through the Devil's Whisper on to the cliff top. Once there she threw herself down on the short, dry turf among a cluster of bright pink thrift, and grinned up at her friend. 'What are you painting?'

'The sea, as usual, but today there's something really magical about it, calm and quiet and drifting along in wonderful colours.' Jane looked down. 'And what are you doing here? Collecting shells, I suppose?' She held up her brush and her smile flowered. 'Charlie,

I must tell you about our call on the Reeds yesterday afternoon. They were so nice. And Bradley . . .'

Charlie watched Jane's pretty face flush with excitement.

'And Bradley, Mr Reed I should say, will be coming to the bazaar, and he showed an interest in my paintings!'

Charlie chipped in, eyes alight with amusement. 'So you have a new beau and you think he might buy one of them?'

'He's not my beau!' The flush spread down Jane's neck.

'Are you sure?' Charlie smiled at her friend. It was good to see Jane excited about something, for she seemed to live a quiet, uneventful life.

Jane concentrated on her painting again. 'Now, Charlie. This afternoon you must put on a very pretty frock and your best bonnet, for Bradley, Mr Reed, is extremely well dressed, and so is his sister, who, for a small woman, looked very elegant, I thought.'

'Hmm,' said Charlie lazily. 'I wonder what the village thinks of them.' But the words meant nothing, for she was thinking of other things, staring out to sea and watching for a sign of Andy's boat returning to the bay.

Jane started packing up her easel and her bag of paints and brushes as it was time to go home for luncheon. 'I'll walk to the village with you,' Charlie said, getting up, 'and tomorrow, when we go to the bazaar, I'll tell you what I thought of Mr Bradley Reed, your new beau.'

Onee again Jane flushed. 'He's not my beau!'

'Not yet perhaps, but I can see you've got your eye on him . . .' Now they both laughed and went on to talk about the bazaar.

They parted at the crossway in the village, Jane continuing along the road to her home and Charlie turning back, climbing the cliff road and on to Headland House.

As they bid goodbye, Jane said, 'Father will call for you in the carriage tomorrow morning, Charlie. He will take us to the bazaar before he goes on his rounds, and collect us later on.' She rearranged the folded easel beneath her arm, and chuckled as she added saucily, 'and be sure not to wear your old breeches—remember to dress properly, won't you?'

Charlie waved her hand. 'I'll do my best, but of course, you'll be the prettiest girl there.'

After luncheon Aunt Jem went to her room to prepare herself for the call on the Reeds, saying to Charlie as she went upstairs, 'Your most becoming dress, please, Charlotte, and that nice new bonnet I bought you the other day. And make sure your hair is tidy, and your gloves clean. And don't keep me waiting . . . the carriage will be ready in fifteen minutes.'

'But it's only a step to The Look Out, Aunt. Surely we can walk?'

'One does not make a social call on foot,

26

child.'

The carriage took exactly four minutes to climb the hill and turn into the drive of The Look Out. Aunt Jem and Charlie were welcomed into the large and imposing hallway then taken to the drawing-room where the two Reed neighbours awaited them.

'Miss Westland, how do you do? So good of you to call. I am Bradley Reed, and this is my sister, Felicia.'

Aunt Jem returned the greeting and introduced Charlie. 'My niece, Charlotte. Also Miss Westland.'

'I am delighted to meet you.' Bradley's voice was attractive, and Charlotte sitting down on the sofa next to her aunt, thought him quite charming. No wonder Jane had fallen for him. But his sister, Miss Felicia Reed, was not at all what she had expected; older than her brother, perhaps in her thirties, small and birdlike, with gleaming, almost black eyes, hair that had once been a lustrous chestnut and was now faded, but adorned with a jeweled net, and tiny, bony fingers bedecked with huge rings.

Such huge stones, thought Charlie, trying not to stare. How do her small fingers carry them? She knew the village would indeed be intrigued by these new owners of The Look Out.

When Miss Felicia spoke, it was her deep, almost masculine voice that made Charlie open her eyes very wide. 'So this is the child who wears men's clothes while sailing off with the young Reddaway boy? Oh yes, we've heard all about it. Disgraceful!' But those dark eyes were laughing, and Charlie had the feeling that perhaps Miss Felicia would have done the same in her youth, given half a chance.

They talked politely for half an hour, discussing the village, the weather, the coming bazaar, and then somehow local smuggling slipped into the conversation.

'Scandalous!' snorted Miss Felicia and looked at her brother, frowning. 'We must keep our eyes and ears open, Bradley, to see if we can't stop it. Far too much brandy being shipped in, and tobacco, too, to say nothing of snuff and silks and laces. And what are the revenue men doing about it? Nothing, from all I hear.'

Aunt Jem looked slightly askance, thought Charlie, watching and listening very intently. Indeed, she saw her aunt finger the handsome lace collar that decorated her dress, and couldn't help wondering where it came from. Or indeed, she reflected guiltily, was there a possibility that the pale blue muslin of the new ballgown being made for her had also being smuggled into the country?

But tea was being brought in, and so the conversation slipped from smuggling to the latest recipe for macaroons. Mr Reed came to offer them to Charlie and bent low over her plate. 'I have heard about your shell work,

Miss Westland, and I look forward to seeing some of it tomorrow at the bazaar.'

'And, of course, you will be able to see Jane Edwards' paintings, Mr Reed.'

Charlie thought he looked far from interested, even although he nodded and said, 'Indeed.' But she noticed that he kept looking at her while tea continued, and when Aunt Jem said it was time to go, he came to Charlie's side, walking with her into the hallway, as Aunt Jem made her farewell to Miss Felicia.

'I hope I shall see more of you, Miss Westland. Do you ride? I am looking forward immensely to exploring the area as I have a new grey which needs constant exercise. You may see me on the cliff path sometimes. If you do, perhaps we might stop and chat? Or would the village take exception to such unconventional behavior?'

He was looking at her with what she realised was amusement and she felt very cross that her adventurous past was in his mind.

She tossed her head and said crisply, 'I have no intention of doing anything which will please the village gossips, Mr Reed.'

He took a step nearer and she felt the power of his tall body, smelled the tang of tobacco about him and the faint smell of pomade on his light, thick hair.

Hastily she walked to the door and was abruptly aware of the fact that she wished to get away from Bradley Reed. Polite, charming and certainly handsome. Yes, he was all of these things, but there was something else about him that she couldn't make out, and didn't like. As she climbed into the carriage behind Aunt Jem, she turned to look back and met his unblinking hazel eyes. She said, 'Goodbye, Mr Reed,' and was thankful when Eddie, the groom, drove them safely back to Headland House.

*   *   *

The barn near the Endacott farm where the church bazaar was being held was prettily decorated with greenery and flowers, and the village ladies had set up small trestle tables, covered with their different wares and crafts. Charlie and Jane arrived in Dr Edwards' carriage and the groom helped carry in their paintings and shell work.

Dr Edwards smiled at them as he climbed back into the carriage, saying jovially, 'I shall come and pick you up well before luncheon, Jane, so be sure you are packed up by then. Good luck, my dears!'

Charlie enjoyed helping Jane set out the table which Mrs Endacott indicated, covering it with a cloth decorated with cream embroidery, and then seeing how their wares looked in various arrangements.

Jane's paintings were propped up by stones

which they found outside in the farm yard, and Charlie set her big bunch of shell flowers on the corner, to be seen clearly by anyone walking around the barn.

The time flew past. Soon the barn was full of people, looking around, chatting and stopping at tables to purchase something that caught their eye. One of Jane's paintings was inspected very carefully by Mr Sealey, the church warden, but although he admired it, no offer was made to buy it. And it wasn't until Bradley Reed and his sister arrived that Jane managed a smile or two.

They stopped by the table and said, 'Good morning,' which both Charlie and Jane acknowledged and returned. Then Jane slipped out from behind her paintings and came to Bradley Reed's side. 'I believe you are fond of the sea, Mr Reed? Well, that is what I love to paint. This one, for instance, shows it in all its powerful fury.'

Charlie, seeing Bradley reply and appear interested, engaged Miss Reed in conversation to give them time together. 'Are you interested in shells, Miss Reed?' she asked.

Felicia Reed looked at her with those penetrating, dark eyes. 'Indeed, I am.' She touched the big Mother Of Pearl in the middle of the arrangement with her tiny, gloved fingers, and went on, 'I see you have a talent for working with them, Miss Westland. And that reminds me that we have a ruined grotto in The Look Out garden. I understand that it needs some work being done on it if we are to keep those lovely shells in their proper place. I am certain . . .' she nodded towards the big flower arrangement in front of her 'that you are the person to do it. What do you say?'

Charlie was surprised, but very interested. To restore the old grotto? She had heard tales of it since childhood, and now, to use all her knowledge of shell work technique would be a most fascinating task. At once she said, 'I should love to do so, Miss Reed. If you think I am capable of it, that is . . .'

The dark eyes gleamed with amusement. 'I think you are capable of most things, Miss Westland. Come for coffee on Monday morning and we'll discuss what needs doing. And now I must move on. Bradley, shall we go and see the pottery display?'

He went, almost like a lamb to the fold, thought Charlie, watching how he cut short his conversation with Jane, and followed his sister around the remaining tables. Bradley Reed was a complex character all right, she told herself, turning back to adjust her shell arrangement.

And then someone came up to the table, stood in front of it, and looked at her. A slim man dressed in shabby clothes, wearing a battered hat that almost completely hid his curling hair but allowed his bright sea-green eyes to shine out. 'Good morning,' he said politely, and smiled.

'Good morning . . .' Charlie felt her heart suddenly leap. She knew those eyes. They were the same ones that had shone in the moonlight; the slender, strong hand that reached out to touch one of the shell flowers the hand that had saluted her the other night.

AN OFFER IS MADE

Charlie, knew she was standing there like a stupid child, with her mouth open and her eyes wide, but had no idea what to do or say. Jane had turned to her and was looking at her curiously, but suddenly the amazing situation resolved itself.

Bradley Reed returned, appearing out of the small groups of people wandering around the barn, and pushed past the shabbily dressed man who still held her gaze.

'Ah, Miss Westland,' he said crisply, his smile full of what appeared to be enjoyment at seeing her. 'I've come to take a good look at your beautiful shell work because my sister tells me she is enlisting your aid in restoring our old grotto. So this is what you do? A most beautiful flower arrangement! I congratulate you.'

Charlie was taken aback, but was too busy looking around for the smiling man who had suddenly disappeared from view. There was no sign of him and she thought he must have slipped away without her noticing.

A huge feeling of disappointment filled her, but now Bradley was touching the shell flowers and asking her questions. With dismay, she made herself concentrate on what he was saying.

'I should like to buy this beautiful arrangement, Miss Westland, for my sister's birthday next month. I know she would enjoy having it in her boudoir. Are you prepared to sell it?'

Charlie knew instantly that she wasn't at all prepared to let the Reeds have the best shell arrangement she had done so far; but Bradley's penetrating eyes were powerful, and almost without knowing, she murmured, 'Yes, of course. I'm glad you like it, but I have no idea of a price.'

His patronising smile would have angered her had she not still been caught up in a haze of confusion. 'But how unsuitable of me to talk about money.' His smile broadened. 'Instead, perhaps you will allow me to make a donation to the church funds?'

Gratefully, she said, 'Why, yes, that would be good of you. Er . . .'

He was standing very close to her with just the narrow table between them and Charlie felt herself shrink as she met those alert eyes. Her voice trembled. 'Would you like to take it now, or perhaps it could be delivered by our groom?'

'Leave it all to me, Miss Westland. I will make arrangements. No need for you to worry about anything. And now I would like to study Miss Edwards' seascapes, particularly the ones she told me about.'

Jane immediately bustled forward, drawing his attention to her pictures, while Charlie stepped back, wondering why she felt so hostile to this pleasant and handsome man. And why she had allowed him—well, not quite, but the idea stayed in her mind—to walk off with her best shell arrangement. Recovering slowly, she accepted the idea that Bradley Reed was a man who knew how to bend people to his own advantage.

Then her mind jumped backwards. He was just the opposite, she knew it most certainly, of the smiling, shabbily dressed man who had said good morning in such a musical, quiet voice before Bradley appeared and spoiled her day. But then she heard Jane describing her pictures, knew from the tone of her voice that she was thoroughly enjoying the moment, and so stood back from the table, trying to sort out her bewildered thoughts.

*　　　*　　　*

True to his word, Dr Edwards appeared later in the morning, by which time Jane and

Charlie had packed up what remained of their goods and were waiting for him.

Jane was delighted with the two sales she had made; and even although Bradley Reed hadn't offered to buy one, he had expressed great interest in her seascapes, saying, 'Clearly, you are a girl who loves the sea, Miss Edwards. Perhaps I might suggest a trip out in my boat one day when the weather is calm and there are no great waves, such as you have painted, to affect our passage?'

Charlie had seen Jane's pale face become suffused with colour and realised that her friend's feelings for Bradley were growing stronger. She wished Jane well, but for herself she thought that nothing Bradley might suggest would interest her. Yet it was clear that Jane needed friendly support, so she whispered to her, 'Go on, say yes. I'll come with you if you like . . .'

'Thank you, Mr Reed. That would be delightful.' Jane's voice had trembled with pleasure and after Bradley had bowed, saying, As soon as we have the right conditions, I will call on your father, Miss Edwards, and arrange a trip,' and then moved away from them.

She turned to Charlie, eyes shining, as she said, 'Oh, Charlie, won't it be lovely? On his boat! I can't wait!'

Very soon Dr Edwards appeared, and they carried their belongings to the waiting carriage. 'A successful morning, my dears?' he asked as they sat opposite him, driving out of the village towards their homes.

Jane said dreamily, 'Yes, Papa. Oh, so very successful.'

It was left to Charlie to say, 'We made a few sales, Dr Edwards, and Mrs Endacott seemed pleased with what we've done.' She smiled mischievously. 'And both of us have received kind invitations—ask Jane what Mr Reed has suggested.'

Dr Edwards frowned, looking at his daughter with careful eyes. 'Well, my dear?'

'A trip in his boat, Papa! When the weather is suitable he will call and arrange it, and Charlie will come as well—do say I may go? Please!'

'I understand that the Reeds are a well-thought-of family and I shall look forward to making his acquaintance when he calls.' Smiling, he nodded. 'Yes, Jane, you may go on this sailing trip, provided Mr Reed assures me that his boat is completely seaworthy and also that he doesn't intend to venture too far afield.'

'Thank you, Papa!' Jane relapsed into dreamy silence, only stirring as the carriage delivered Charlie to Headland House.

Charlie thanked Dr Edwards, told Jane she would be seeing her again soon, and watched the carriage roll away. She carried the remains of her shell work into the house and met Aunt Jem in the hallway.

'I am going to help restore the shell grotto at The Look Out, Aunt. Miss Reed has asked me to do so and I expect Mr Reed will call to make arrangements. Isn't it exciting?'

Aunt Jem pursed her lips. 'What, that ruined dark old place? Certainly not! Too many tales connected with it, as I remember something about a jewel being stolen, I think. Really, Charlotte, how extraordinary to ask you to do such a menial job—does she not have a gardener or an odd job man who could do it?'

Charlie felt some of her happiness fade away. 'Yes, I expect she does, or if not, perhaps Papa would let Mr Reddaway come and help me with the heavy work when he's not too busy in our own garden, but I can certainly deal with the restoration of the shells.' She looked at her aunt very firmly, and added before an reply could be given, 'So Aunt, I shall need to go down to the beach this afternoon and collect whatever the tide has brought in—just for an hour before tea. Please may I go?'

A heavy sigh and then a growing smile. 'What a defiant creature you are, with your enthusiasms! Yes, I suppose you can go and collect shells, but you must ask your papa at luncheon and see what he says about the restoration idea. Now, hurry up and put away all that clobber . . .'

It wasn't clobber, thought Charlie crossly, climbing the stairs and putting all her beautiful shells and what was left of her small arrangements on the table below the window in her bedroom. And then washed her hands, tidied her hair, and went down to luncheon to hear what Papa had to say.

He thought for a long moment, frowning a little, but then turned to Charlie, sitting at the side of the long table, and asked slowly, 'Do you really have enough experience to work with shells in the old grotto, Charlotte? Yes, you certainly make very pretty arrangements, but this will surely necessitate some building of the old walls and so on.' He paused, looking solemn, as he added, 'and there are some unpleasant stories about the grotto in the past, so I'm not sure whether you should be there alone.'

Charlie said quickly, 'Yes, I know all about that, Papa, and if Mr Reed doesn't already have a gardener, I thought you could lend him Mr Reddaway when he's not too busy here? He can help with the rough work, and keep me safe.' She concealed her chuckle, thinking that perhaps Andy would come and help, too, when he wasn't fishing. 'And another thing,' she went on hurriedly, 'I'm quite sure I shall be able to restore the old shells and even replace them with new ones.'

Mr Westland looked at her fondly. 'Yes, you may go, but I need to meet Mr Reed before you do so.'

'I think he is planning to call on you and Dr Edwards very soon.' Charlie made no mention of the boat trip; one thing at a time, she thought sensibly.

'I look forward to meeting him. I'll mention that we could lend Reddaway for a short time if necessary. I suppose you will be collecting shells this afternoon?'

'Yes,' said Charlie happily.

'Well,' said her papa firmly, 'just remember what we talked about the other night. No breeches and boots, if you please.'

Subdued laughter from Aunt Jem helped Charlie join in, and the meal ended happily.

About to go to her room to slip into an old dress which wouldn't mind getting sea stained, Charlie was stopped in the hallway by the kitchen maid. 'Please, Miss, Andy Reddaway came round just now and left something for you.'

'Oh! What did he leave, Susie?'

'A bucket of crabs, Miss, and an old tin trunk. Cook's taken the crabs into the kitchen and the trunk is just outside the back door. Shall I bring it in?'

Well done, Andy, thought Charlie gratefully. Her disguise of breeches and boots would be tucked away safely in her room without anyone knowing they were there. Not that she intended to wear them, of course, but one never knew what the future might hold . . .

'Thank you, Susie. Just bring the trunk up to my room and I'll decide what to do with it.' She skipped upstairs, changed her dress, put on an old bonnet, collected the shell bag and was about to leave again when the trunk came, heaved up the stairs by a breathless Susie. 'Not very heavy, Miss. I wonder what's in it; treasure, do you think?'

Susie's eyes were full of wonder and Charlie laughed. 'Not now, but perhaps it was once upon a time. Yes, put it there in the corner and I'll see to it later.'

With the trunk pushed against the wall, opened and her disguise taken out and hidden beneath her usual clothes in drawers and wardrobe, Charlie finally left her room and headed for the beach. Her spirits were high. Clearly Andy hadn't forgotten her. It was kind of him to have retrieved her old clothes from the cave, found an excuse of delivering crabs and so returning them to her.

The beach was empty and the sea very quiet, lapping prettily on the sand in lacy patterns as the tide slowly turned.

Charlie knew she had an hour or two before the dried-out lines of driftwood, seaweed and shells left from the morning tide were once again submerged, so she bent to the task, thinking of little else save what she was looking for and enjoying the fresh sea air, the music of the waves and the lingering scent of salt.

There were plenty of small shells; winkles,

tiny cowries, cockles, limpets, periwinkles. Of course, she only found the ordinary ones, but her mind remembered the lovely top shells and razor shells and just a few of the lovely orange-banded dog whelks she had in her room at home.

As she searched slowly along the beach, eyes intent on the jetsam that littered the sand, she thought she heard the sound of crunching footsteps. Then, looking up, she saw someone had just climbed down from the Devil's Whisper cave, over the big, black rocks that turned into shingle as they reached the tide line. Her first thought was Andy, but no, she stood up straight, squinting into the sun which shone in her eyes and was delighted to hear a familiar voice saying quietly, 'Good afternoon.'

Her heart jumped. Here was the smuggler, the man who had bidden her good morning at the bazaar, and then vanished. What was he doing here? And what was he saying?

'If you're looking for shells, then you'll have to come out in my boat and visit some foreign beaches. Over the seas you'll find great conches, and shells that never come here. How I should like to sail off with you and find them.'

His eyes were as blue-green as the sea beneath summer sun, and startlingly bright. Who was he?

At her side now he bent down and lifted a strand of seaweed, picking up a scallop shell hiding beneath it. 'You missed this one,' he said, smiling. 'I think I'd better help you, hadn't I?'

Charlie shook her head at such impertinence but could think of nothing to say; until, suddenly, words rushed out without thought. 'You were riding down the cliff path by our house the other night. You were carrying packages and what looked like small kegs.'

'Yes.' He nodded and continued looking down at the tide line. 'Taking brandy and some tobacco to certain people in the village. The vicar likes us to come at night—and so does the magistrate, your papa. You weren't meant to be awake at that time.' He raised his head and grinned at her shocked expression. 'Young ladies need their beauty sleep, don't they? Although . . .' He stopped, his smile died and his voice dropped as he continued quietly, 'You, Miss Westland, are so pretty, that I don't think you need sleep so long. Perhaps a trip around the bay one evening might do you even more good—what do you say?'

But Charlie had recovered herself. She said sharply, '1 say that you are being extremely personal and rude, and I don't wish to have anything more to do with you.'

The sea-green eyes softened and looked at her with a new expression. Gone was the sauciness, and instead Charlie saw tenderness in them, as he said, almost inaudibly, 'Oh, but

43

I think you do, Miss Charlie. I know about your adventures, you see, and I know you kept secret the fact that you saw us the other night. And this morning, at the bazaar, you didn't give me away, did you?'

Charlie thought she had stopped breathing as she realised she was suddenly at the start of a new adventure. She smiled at the lean face watching her so keenly and asked unsteadily, 'You know my name, but what is yours?'

'Ned,' he said, vivid eyes full of amusement. 'And that's all I'm going to tell you. For the moment . . .'

Charlotte sucked in a huge breath and said unsteadily, 'But I know you're a smuggler. I saw you, with the barrels and kegs . . .'

Ned took a step nearer to her, put the shell he was holding into her bag, and then said, very quietly and with what she thought was a mischievous smile, 'I think you should forget all about that, Miss Westland.'

'Charlie,' she whispered, all convention gone, caught up in the wonder of the moment and wishing it could go on for ever.

'Charlie, then. Although you don't look like a cabin boy dressed in breeches, which is the gossip I've heard in the village. If I may say so, you are a very beautiful young lady.'

'Oh!' Charlie was at a loss but felt warmth rush through her body. She had, of course, received compliments before, but none had struck home so deeply and excitingly as Ned's last words. Then her smile faded. Was he, perhaps, merely teasing her? Certainly, he seemed a mysterious person who might well simply be amusing himself.

So she stood up very straight, gathered together her bag of shells, thought of Aunt Jem, and decided this was enough for the afternoon. This man was playing games, she was sure of it, and she had other things to think about. Smuggling, talking about sailing off to foreign lands to find shells—indeed, even taking her with him—what nonsense!

'Good afternoon,' she said crisply, turning away and leaving him standing there, watching as she went as quickly as she could down the beach and on towards Headland House.

As she went, she complimented herself on behaving sensibly. Aunt Jem would be proud of her, she thought, but even as she reached the cliff path, something made her turn and look over her shoulder.

He was standing there; a dark sunlit figure, his wild hair blowing slightly in the breeze, hat in hand. The mysterious stranger, Ned, was watching and waiting . . .

*   *   *

Bradley Reed called next morning. Charlie heard him arrive, knew Papa was taking him into his study and offering him chocolate or coffee, or even perhaps a glass of Madeira.

45

It all depended whether he liked him or not. She saw Susie arrive with glasses, and listened, without seeming to do so, by loitering on the stairs, and hoping that, as the Madeira was being offered, the call must be going well.

A little later, Bradley came out escorted by Papa who was talking about the gardener.

'We've had Pete Reddaway for many years,' he told his visitor. 'He's quite reliable, and is knowledgeable, too. I'm sure you'll be glad of his help, but don't keep him too long, please.' Papa's voice held a smile. 'I shall need him back here before mid summer when the roses start to fall, you know! My sister gets very impatient with all those fallen petals.'

And then Bradley's voice. 'Most kind of you, Mr Westland. I appreciate it, and of course I'll reimburse the man myself for all he does. Now we must talk about your charming daughter, who is going to work her magic on the old shells.'

'Yes,' said Papa, looking up the staircase. 'And I think she's probably around here somewhere, if you'd like a word with her. Charlotte?' he called loudly from the hallway.

Charlie paused a moment before slipping out from behind the far banister at the end of the passage. 'Yes, Papa. Do you want me?'

'My dear, Mr Reed is here and wishes to discuss the shell work with you. Come along down, will you? We'll go into the garden and I'll speak to Reddaway.'

46

Before she knew it, Charlie was alone on the terrace, with Papa striding down to the vegetable patch, leaving Bradley to smile at her and say how deliciously pretty she looked today.

'Thank you:' said Charlie impatiently, looking away. 'But what I really want is to know when I can begin work on the grotto. If Mr Reddaway is free this afternoon, why don't we make a start?' She thought Bradley looked at her with raised eyebrows, but then saw him nod and smile.

'An excellent idea. If you can come after luncheon, I shall have had time to get the old place tidied up a little and a lamp ready for our exploration. It should be a most interesting project.'

'But . . .' She hadn't realised that he would want to be with her. However, she was quite sure that Bradley, with his smart clothes, wouldn't stay very long among those old and dirty stones. 'I look forward to it, Mr Reed,' she told him and then saw his expression change, knowing at once that he was going to ask a favour. She was right.

'I hope you will call me by my given name, Miss Charlotte. After all, we're going to spend some time together in this little project, aren't we? So surely we could become friends? What do you say?'

He had stepped closer to her and without thinking, she stepped back, saying hesitantly,

'Well, of course, Mr Reed. I mean Bradley, if that is what you want . . .'

'I do. Yes, I do, Charlotte. There, now you see how easily your name trips off my tongue. We are friends, then. I am delighted that we are going to spend some time together.'

Charlie stiffened. He was being far too friendly for her liking. He must be put in his place. 'But I am quite capable of restoring the shell work on my own, Mr, er, Bradley, with Mr Reddaway's help, of course. You see, I shan't need anyone to be with me.'

She met his intense gaze and was surprised at the flash of darkness in his eyes. Was it anger? But almost at once he smiled again, and said lightly, 'I can see you're a lady who enjoys hard work, Charlotte, but perhaps I shall be allowed to hold a trowel or even hand you some shells from time to time? I want to make myself useful, you see.'

Thank goodness she saw Papa coming up the garden with Mr Reddaway beside him. Hurriedly, she said, 'Oh yes, I'm sure there will little jobs you can help me with,' and then turned quickly to find Papa at her side.

'Well, here is your helper, Mr Reed, ready and willing to do what he can for your old grotto.' Papa smiled and nodded at Pete Reddaway, standing there, as solid and silent as usual, but grinning at Bradley and raising a finger to his cap as if to assure him of his willingness to help out.

48

'Excellent,' said Bradley, bestowing a tight smile on the gardener and then turning back to Charlotte and her father. 'So let us say we will make a start this afternoon. Reddaway, come at two-thirty and I'll show you where the tools are kept. No doubt you will need to make some mortar, which we will think about tomorrow, but this afternoon we'll just survey the old place and make our plans.'

Charlie felt her heart sinking. Bradley was taking over the whole project, yet it was she whom Miss Felicia had invited to do the work. She looked at her father, who was watching her and, she guessed, sensed very well that she was disappointed at the way things were working out. But Bradley was making his farewells, and so she could only accompany him to the gate where the pony and trap waited, and then watch him drive up the hill, giving a last wave as he went.

'All right, Reddaway,' said Papa, turning back to the waiting gardener. 'Keep on with weeding the peas, will you? And this afternoon you can accompany Miss Charlotte to The Look Out.'

He looked at Charlotte as they walked slowly back to the house. 'I can see you are upset by him planning to take over your work, but, my dear, you must realise that Mr Reed, being a gentleman, is very anxious to make the work as easy as he can.'

Charlie felt her face blaze. She came to

49

a decisive stop, and turned to her father. 'No, Papa! Miss Felicia has given me the responsibility of restoring the grotto!'

Silence for a moment, and then she added, seeing her father conceal a smile, 'and anyway, I don't like him. He's not someone I want to get to know any better.'

Her father opened the door and followed her into the hallway. 'Well, what a pity, is all I can say. From what I gather from village talk and those who know his family, Bradley Reed is a sensible young man with excellent prospects in the woolen trade—he owns an estate up country, I understand—and perhaps might be a possible suitor for you, Charlotte, my dear.'

She stared at him, astounded. 'Never! Papa, please don't even think such a thing!'

He shook his head, and then glanced at the grandfather clock, striking the hour. 'But come, dear child, don't be upset, it's early days yet. And now I think we must go and tell your Aunt Jemima exactly what is happening.'

Aunt Jemima was closing her desk, some envelopes in her hand. 'Ah, Charlotte, perhaps you would be kind enough to drive down into the village and post these letters for me. Ask Eddie to get out the trap, will you?'

Charlie had no wish at all to leave the house. She had plenty to think about and prepare ready for the afternoon's work. But, sighing, she said, 'Yes, Aunt, I'll go at once.'

As they trotted down into the village, she was glad she was there after all. The sun shone, the distant sea lilted as it flowed into the bay, hungry gulls called. All so different from this coming afternoon when she would have to find her way, with Bradley's help, of course, into the old grotto which would most likely be dark and musty.

Her mind roamed backwards. What could she remember of the childhood tales about the place? She turned to Eddie beside her. 'Do you know anything about the grotto at the Manor House, Eddie?'

He frowned, giving her a sideways glance 'Dirty ol' place, Miss Charlotte. We used to play there as boys, but it weren't really safe. Lots of fallen stones, and so dark and damp. And then, those ol' noises, footsteps, like. Why, I remember Davey Young swearin' that he'd seen a ghost down there. A young lady who was crossed in love, they say. Mind you, Davey was always imaginin' things. But I did hear a ring was found and then stolen . . .' Eddie's expression was anxious as he brought the trap to a halt in the village square. 'Not thinkin' of goin' there, are you, Miss Charlotte? No, that'd never do . . . not safe, not safe at all.'

Charlie felt a twist of something between excitement and fright spread through her as she got out of the trap and went to post the letters. So the grotto was haunted? Was that what Eddie meant? Footsteps, and a ghost, and a lost ring. Just for a few seconds, while she watched the letters disappear into the postbox, Charlie wondered at the adventure that lay ahead of her. But when she turned back to mount the trap, she was as brave as ever. After all, adventures were what made her life so exciting and lively.

As Eddie clucked to the pony and started off up the hill again, she smiled to herself. Even if there was a ghost, at least she would have Bradley Reed to protect her. And then a wonderful new thought followed on; she could ask Bradley to ghost hunt while she got on with the shell work. Yes, that would get rid of his bothering presence for a good long while.

She was chuckling to herself when she returned to the house, to find Jane waiting, chatting to Aunt Jem on the terrace.

Jane sprang up, full of smiles. 'Charlie, I mean,' She slid an apologetic glance at Aunt Jem's raised eyebrows. 'Charlotte, I have some very good news.'

'What is it?' Charlie thought Jane was looking excited.

'The Reeds have sent a message to Father asking him for permission to take me on a trip in their schooner! Fancy! Did you know they had one? How rich they must be!'

'Oh,' said Charlie, thoughtfully. A schooner? Jane was right, the Reeds must be very wealthy. 'And what about me? Am I included in the invitation?'

'Of course! Father said I must have a companion, and so I've come straight away to ask you as he wants to reply to Bradley, I mean Mr and Miss Reed, tomorrow morning, so tell me your answer quickly, and don't dare say no!'

Charlie looked at Aunt Jem who put down her embroidery frame and cleared her throat, obviously having thoughts about the matter.

'My dear Jane,' she started, 'we don't really know these people very well, do we? What does your father think about the invitation? Very kind, certainly, but a little, well, definitely unconventional. I mean two young ladies out there in a large boat, with the sea and the weather all around them, and only rough sailors accompanying them . . .'

'Oh no, Miss Westland,' laughed Jane, sitting down beside Charlie. 'The invitation is from Miss Felicia actually, and she says that we shall be quite comfortable and safe, and that our families have nothing to worry about. What fun it will be. I shall take my paints and try to get a true picture of the very large waves . . .'

'And I,' said Charlie, grinning, 'will look for shells where ever we moor up. We're bound to go into one of the little coves for a picnic.'

'We could even swim!' But Jane's exuberance was soon quelled as Aunt Jem coughed loudly.

53

'I think we must wait for Dr Edwards and my brother to decide whether the invitation is to be accepted or not, young ladies. And now, tell me, Jane, how your garden grows. We are having such trouble this year with greenfly on the roses . .'

Charlie and Jane at last managed to escape from the terrace and went up to Charlie's bedroom where they sat on the bed and laughed. 'Swim! Mix with the sailors! Hear some of their wicked language? Be seasick? Oh yes, of course we must go . . .'

Jane calmed down at last and said quietly and shyly, 'But it will be lovely, with Bradley there, looking after us. He is such a pleasant man, don't you think so, Charlie?'

Charlie waited long enough to see Jane's eyes grow anxious, and then said firmly, 'I don't care for him quite as you clearly do, Jane, but perhaps you know him better than I do.' She watched her friend nod, and then added, 'This afternoon he is going to take me into the old grotto to make plans for its restoration. I'm sure I shall know a lot more about him after an hour or so in his company'

'An hour or so?' To her discomfort, Jane just stared at her, eyes narrowed, and a look of—could it be jealousy, thought Charlie, painfully?—on her small, pretty face. After a moment's uncomfortable silence she said curtly, 'Well, I must go now, Charlie. Don't bother to see me out.' She ran down the stairs

54

and out to the waiting gig before Charlie could
say anything more.

A SECRET MEETING

It was exactly two o'clock when, when, with a
crunch of gravel, Bradley Reed drew his trap
to a halt outside Headland House. Charlie
was standing by the window in the drawing-
room, so waited until Susie had announced
the visitor, and Bradley came in, smiling
handsomely, with his hat in his hand, and
saying, 'Here I am, then, Charlotte, ready to
take you up to The Look Out. And then we'll
explore the old grotto. I have a lamp lit inside
and a good supply of candles.'

Charlie nodded, not knowing quite what to
say. She watched his eyes glint as he looked at
her, assessing her dress. 'Such a pretty gown.
I hope you won't get any dirty marks on it.
Perhaps a wrapper, or something, do you
think?'

Goodness, thought Charlie, instantly
enraged—anyone would think he was already
her husband, ordering her about. She turned
away sharply, saying as she headed for the
door, 'I'm quite capable of choosing my dress
and avoiding dirt, Bradley. No wrapper, thank
you. Now, shall we go?'

He looked askance at the big bag of shells

55

waiting in the hallway, but she was ready for him. 'They're not heavy. Perhaps you could put them in the trap.'

He drove the trap far too fast for Charlie's liking, but she maintained a controlled silence as they rushed up the hill and through the village. Then Charlie's eyes opened wide, for there, standing on the cliff path, talking to a group of men, and today dressed in smart breeches, white shirt, black jacket and holding his tricorn hat, was Ned, the smuggler. But why was he dressed like that?

Charlie looked back over her shoulder. Why, he's wearing a uniform, and at that moment Bradley followed her glance, took one look at the man they were passing and said, almost contemptuously, 'Ah, a Riding Officer! So this is how the Preventive men spend their time when they're not at the Customs House— gossiping instead of watching for incoming vessels. No wonder they never catch any smugglers.'

Without thinking, Charlie said sharply, 'but he's not a Preventive Officer, he's . . .' and then bit off the words for Bradley was looking at her with searching eyes. 'I mean,' she floundered, and then stopped.

'You mean that you have seen him before?' Bradley's voice was suddenly sharp and Charlie's mind quickened. She must definitely not allow Bradley to suspect anything about Ned, no matter if he really was a smuggler.

She said, as casually as she could manage, 'You don't remember, obviously, but he was admiring my shell arrangement at the bazaar before you and your sister arrived. Now, can we please get on? I want to start work on the grotto before the afternoon disappears completely.'

Bradley made no reply, but she saw from his sour expression that he wasn't pleased with her explanation and she felt relieved as he whipped up the pony and trotted along the road leading to The Look Out. At the front entrance, he dismounted, flung the reins to the waiting groom and then offered Charlie his hand.

'I can manage, thank you.' She stepped down unaided. 'But you might carry the bag of shells.' His obvious annoyance was enjoyable, and she at once started off down the garden path in front of him. 'Is this the way to the grotto? I expect I shall see Mr Reddaway waiting for me.'

He was there, of course, touching his cap as she arrived and saying, 'Well, Miss Charlotte, 'tis a dirty ol' place all right, but there's a lantern inside and some candles. Shall I show you the way in?'

'Yes, please, Mr Reddaway. I'm really excited about it.'

She walked with him towards a large and neglected-looking grey stone building half covered in ivy, with a small open doorway, ignoring Bradley's words that followed her. 'Charlotte, please wait. Allow me to conduct you around.'

But she couldn't wait. Pete Reddaway held up a lantern as they approached the dark doorway, and said, over his shoulder, 'Watch yer feet, Miss Charlotte, 'tis pebbles and dirt all over?'

Charlie said nothing. As she went into the darkness, she followed the gleaming lantern light and sucked in her breath. She had thought a grotto was just a stone cave, often decorated with shells.

Nothing had prepared her for all this, for here she was in a veritable cavern, tall built with arches and high walls, and as Pete Reddaway moved the lantern around, she saw that every surface was covered with shells. Not just shells though, but—she put a hand on his arm. 'Stop here for a minute, Mr Reddaway,' and then, looking closely at the covered wall, recognised shining pieces of mica, feathers arranged in wonderful designs, as well as every shell that she had ever heard of, and, indeed, some that she had never seen before. Beautiful shapes and forms and colours. Where had they all come from?

Bradley was calling loudly, and she knew she could no longer ignore him. His voice boomed mysteriously through the empty darkness, 'Charlotte, I think you should stay here in the entrance cave, it's far too dangerous to go any further, if, indeed, one can. Reddaway, give me the lantern and go and light some candles. Got a tinder box, have you?'

'Yes, sir.' Pete Reddaway handed over the lantern with what Charlie saw was reluctance and a last glance back at her. For a moment his body shielded the light from the entrance and she realised what complete darkness was like, but then Bradley was at her side, holding up the lantern and pointing at a decoration on one of the walls. 'Here are some of your beloved shells, Charlotte. You can see how damaged they are. Will you be able to repair this panel?'

She stared at it. A tall panel was set into a background of what looked like ordinary clam shells and periwinkles, but the panel was very different; very rich, both in pattern and colour, even though fading and neglect were plain. It depicted a flower with a large head and a long stem about which leaves uncurled. Excitement filled her. 'Shine the light here, please, Bradley. I must look at this.'

It was beautiful, so well shaped and with an abundance of shells of all sizes and colours forming the tall, elegant flower. Charlie stared, wide-eyed and then slowly, as the image connected with another one already in her head, whispered, 'It's a rose, that beautiful head of unfurling petals, those great leaves, and that wonderful golden centre. Why, I can almost smell its fragrance.'

Bradley was at her side now, and she felt him watching, listening to her rapturous words.

'A rose? Are you sure? But why should anyone want to depict a rose growing in a dark cave like this?'

'I don't know.' Yet she knew one thing, that she already loved this decoration, and knew she must keep it to herself. She reached out a hand and ran her fingers over the shape in front of her, and then dropped her hand as she reached the golden centre of the flower.

She recognised the tiny, yellow winkle shells, all arranged in pristine form, outlining the central thrust of the stamens of the flower. They were ordinary shells, but, despite their age and covering dirt, they gleamed as the lantern light shone on them.

Charlie held her breath and fingered them. And as she did so, she felt something give in the centre of the circle, as if there might be a hole beneath the ancient shells. A sense of something strange filled her mind. First this lovely rose created in the complete darkness, and then the possibility of a concealed hole—a hiding place, perhaps? Something made her decide rapidly to keep all of this to herself. She had no idea why this seemed so important, but quickly she said, 'Shall we look at the other walls?' and stepped away from the panel.

Yes, there were plenty of decorations on all the walls they looked at. Lantern light showed up birds in flight, ships on crashing waves, trees and mountains, houses and small shapes which suggested other tiny decorative flowers, but nothing quite as eye catching as the huge rose on the wall opposite the entrance.

By the time Pete Reddaway had returned and managed to fix lighted candles into a couple of ancient, rather broken sconces on the far walls, she was eager to get rid of Bradley and start work. There was so much to be done here—cleaning, removing broken shells, finding new ones that would exactly fit and enhance the original decorations. She felt her heart race with excitement.

So how to get rid of Bradley, who hovered at her side which ever way she turned, where ever she looked? Ideas crowded into her mind; perhaps she might ask for a drink?

Surprisingly, though, it was Bradley himself who had the answer. 'If you're sure you feel safe here, Charlotte, I will go and fetch my sister. I know she will want to see these wonders and especially this amazing flower. Perhaps with her experience of travel abroad when she was younger, she may even have some knowledge that might help us to understand what once went on in this dark, dirty place.'

'Yes, please do, Bradley. I shall be quite safe with Mr Reddaway, so don't hurry back.'

As he left, Charlie returned to the tall panel, concentrated on it, and began planning just how she could restore the shells to their full beauty. She must discover why the mortar beneath the shells felt so soft and crumbling. She gestured Pete Reddaway to her side. 'What do you think of this mortar?' she asked. 'Does it need renewing, or can you patch some of the holes if I take out the old shells?'

He scratched his head. 'I'll have to make a trial boring, Miss Charlotte, afore I can tell you that.' Already he was fingering the mortar which crumbled between some of the shells.

'Yes, please do.' She watched him working, slowly and infinitely carefully removing one or two of the most damaged shells and then bending forward, with the lantern held up to his eyes, to see the state of the wall beneath.

'It's very soft in the middle,' breathed Charlie, and then she saw a hole emerging from the falling mortar, a circular shaped hole which seemed lined with something. 'Look!' she said, and together they peered through the lantern light. The hole was round and strong, its walls formed from something other than shells. Charlie's fingers stroked and her mind raced. Finally, 'it's very hard,' she said, and looked at Pete Reddaway.

He nodded slowly. 'This hole's been made out of something strong and unbreakeable. I wonder why?'

'A place to hide things in, perhaps.' Charlie's mind was working overtime and instinct began offering possible facts. The more she thought about it, the more obvious it seemed, that no-one would know that the centre of the rose covered what was virtually a small, strong safe. But someone had made it. Someone had used it. It had been vitally important to hide something precious and secret, and she had found it! Oh, if only she knew what the secret hiding place had contained . . . and why . . .

Pete Reddaway was working away removing mortar and cleaning up the surface of the flower. He glanced sideways at her, and she saw his eyes twinkle. 'All the ol' tales 'bout this place said there was treasure somewhere, Miss Charlie. Left by the poor young lady who loved the man who did all this, but couldn't marry him.'

She froze. The puzzle was beginning to make sense. Treasure stored for safety. A jewel, Aunt Jem had suggested, hidden in a dark cave, with old tales told to frighten people away. And now she was here and she knew she must somehow fit the pieces together. 'Mr Reddaway,' she whispered urgently. 'Let's keep this a secret.'

He nodded. 'I'll do whatever you want me to do, Miss Charlotte. You can rely on me.'

'I know I can. Thank you, Mr Reddaway. But now—' She stopped and turned to look towards the entrance. Voices approached. At once Charlie dived into her bag of shells and picked out some which she thought could fit into the empty spaces of the rose head. She was busily pressing new shells into the mortar as Bradley ushered his sister though the small entrance.

'Well, here we are,' he said and took the lantern from Pete Reddaway, holding it high so that his sister could look around.

'What an extraordinary place,' said Miss Felicia in her deep voice. She pulled her shawl closer about her small body. 'I don't think we want to spend much time in here, such damp, unhealthy air, but I must see the flower you mentioned. Bradley, over here, is it?'

But Bradley had wandered away, leaving the lantern in Pete Reddaway's hands, and seemingly exploring the remainder of the grotto.

Standing just behind Charlie, Miss Felicia bent forward for a long moment, staring at the pearly coloured rose, watching as new shells were painstakingly being pressed into mortar to make up the empty spaces caused by age and neglect.

'I have seen grottos before in Europe,' she said at last, 'but they were far more beautiful and interesting, and full of pools and fountains and so forth. Much more decorative than this rather gloomy place, which is not so intriguing as I had hoped and possibly not so exciting for you, Miss Westland. You certainly won't want to spend much time in here.'

'But I do, Miss Reed,' Charlie had no time to order her thoughts. She met Miss Felicia's deep-set eyes that looked at her so curiously, and then added, 'It will be a real challenge, you see, to reinstate this beautiful flower.'

By now Bradley had returned, and interrupted her flow of words. 'Oh, come, Charlotte, there must be many other far more interesting creative things for you to do than to spend time in here, getting cold and picking up who knows what miasmas and infections from the past.'

Charlie thought she noticed a strange glance being exchanged between brother and sister, and wondered what they were thinking. He continued, 'I don't think any of us will want to come in here again. Now I suggest we go out into the sunshine and think about some tea in the gazebo.' He turned to Pete Reddaway. 'You can carry on with what you are doing, and I think that will be all I shall need. No need to come another day, my man. But make sure you clear up before you leave.'

Charlie's disappointment was enormous, but she had no reason for arguing with him. So slowly she packed up her bag of shells, met Pete Reddaway's knowledgeable eyes, and allowed him to carry the bag out of the grotto and put into the trap, waiting in the stable yard.

Then, disheartened, she followed Miss Felicia and Bradley down the winding path to the wooden gazebo at the bottom of the garden. Miss Felicia sat down and smiled encouragingly. 'Call for tea, Bradley,' she ordered, 'and Miss Westland and I will talk over the flower she has been so cleverly trying to restore. I can't imagine why a rose, after all, quite an ordinary and common flower, should be set into a dark, gloomy grotto, can you, my dear?'

Charlie could only shake her head and so the conversation switched to more everyday matters, but as they sipped tea and nibbled at angel cake, her mind was still engaged with that strange, fascinating and secret hole hidden so well beneath the beautiful rose head.

*   *   *

By the time Charlie left the Manor House, she had been told quite plainly by both Bradley and his sister, that she must spend no more time in the grotto. The reason, they said, was that it was an unhealthy place and no-one would be using it, so why bother about the restoration of the old shells?

But Charlie dared to argue. 'I'm so terribly disappointed that you should say that, Miss Felicia. I was looking forward very much to working in there. Please say that you will allow me to come, well, perhaps for an hour every day? I shall be quite safe with the lantern and the candles.'

She stopped, caught her breath, and then

66

added slowly, and very reluctantly, 'and perhaps Bradley would drop by occasionally to see that I was all right.' The very thing, of course, she wished to avoid, but it seemed the only way of continuing to work on that gorgeous flower.

Bradley's smile told her the trick had worked. 'Well, if that's how you feel, Charlotte, of course you can continue to come. I applaud your hard work. Don't you agree, Felicia?' Receiving a doubtful nod, he added, 'and, don't worry, I shall be there to make sure you are safe.'

So it was arranged, and after Bradley had driven her home to Headland House, Charlie reported to Aunt Jem about the grotto, saying only that the place was a ruin and needed a lot of work.

The rose, of course, was the most important picture in her mind's eye. Had someone created it as a source of light in that dark, unhealthy old place?' Or had the sculptor created it as a sort of message? Roses, of course, were symbols of love. What had Pete Reddaway said? That a young lady living at the Manor had once loved the sculptor, but had been unable to marry him? Then what of Pete Reddaway's words about the tales of treasure being hidden there and the ghost of the poor young lady.

What was her name, Charlie wondered, lying awake in her bed, staring into the dusky shadows of her room, enjoying the pictures which flashed through her mind. Then suddenly all the imaginary pictures crashed down into nothingness, and she sat up in bed, tense with alarm.

A whistle beneath the window. Who ever . . .? She was up, pulling her wrapper around her shoulders, feet bare on the polished boards and pushing the window further ajar so that she could look down through the frame. There, in the half light of the drowsing garden stood a horse, and standing by its side, holding the reins, and looking up at the window, was Ned.

Charlie caught her breath and then experienced a surge of excitement. Was he the smuggler tonight, or the Revenue Officer she thought she had seen this afternoon? Only one way to find out; she leaned as far through the window frame as she could manage, and whispered, 'Who are you?'

The reply was rapid and accompanied by a smile. 'Come down and find out.'

'I couldn't possibly do that,' she said quickly, but Ned's smile grew and then the invitation became too inviting to reject.

'I dare you, Miss Charlie. You won't say no to an adventure, surely?'

The house was quiet, just a few soft snores from Papa's room and some coughs from the attic where Cook and the maids slept. Charlie heard the stairs creak as carefully, treading

68

only on the sides of the steps, she crept down into the hall, unbolted the door and then slipped out into the cool night air.

He was there, a tall dark figure just outside the door, his horse hitched to the elm tree further down the garden. 'Miss Charlie—well done.' His smile made her feel weak; his voice was low and quiet yet as vibrant as a favourite melody 'Where can we go to talk?'

She was confused, but full of excitement. 'In the summer house. Down there, the other side of the pool.' Skirts held up with one hand, cloak wrapped around her, she ran across the lawn, between the long summer borders, and around the dark, whispering lake to the shadowy summer house beneath the copse of birch trees.

Then, in the privacy of the shadowy little house, she turned and faced him. Her heart was racing. Who was he, this man who came only at night and suggested unseemly adventures? Was she being foolish coming here, alone with him, in the darkness? What did he want of her?

But then all the anxieties vanished the moment he took her hand and led her to one of the chairs standing behind them.

'Sit down, Miss Charlie,' he breathed. She sank into the chair, watching as he pulled the other one beside her and folded himself into it. Then he turned to her, smiled, and said, very quietly, 'I can't tell you who I am. Not yet. But

I hope that for the moment you are prepared to trust me. I mean you no harm—indeed, I take the liberty of hoping that you might even enjoy my company when I tell you why I have asked you to come and talk to me tonight.'

She felt this was the moment of decision. To turn back, or go forward? Yes, she knew in some strange way that she could indeed trust him; it flashed briefly through her busy mind that she trusted Ned, this stranger, far more willingly than she could ever say the same of Bradley Reed.

He leaned closer and as if he read her thoughts, he took her hand. His was warm and heavy, the fingers slender but strong and she sat back, calm and delighted.

'Who do you think I am, Miss Charlie?' He sounded a little anxious, she thought.

At once she sought to reassure him, replying, 'A smuggler, of course. You appear at night, riding a horse, with some men who carry kegs of brandy and other things.' Her voice dwindled a little. 'But I'm not sure, you see, because this afternoon I saw you in the uniform of a Revenue Officer.'

She looked at him through the shadowy half light and was thankful to see a gleam of a smile in his bright eyes.

'A Preventive Officer? Who, me? Oh come, Miss Charlie, surely you were dreaming, because, as you've just said, you really think that I'm one of those wicked smugglers, don't you?'

'Oh!' She was at a loss. For a smuggler was a bad man, and Ned couldn't possibly be that bad, could he?

She thought for a long moment and then asked, 'What will happen if you are caught? Will you . . .' she caught her breath, 'be sent to gaol?'

Ned laughed. 'Of course not! Smugglers are friends of ordinary people, bringing them goods which they can't really afford, so they're doing a good turn to everybody. And no magistrate would ever condemn a local smuggler.'

His voice dropped very low. 'Even your father, Miss Charlie; a good man he is, and a very fair magistrate, but because we bring him his brandy, oh, yes, and laces for your lady aunt—he wouldn't dream of punishing us.'

Charlie's head was swimming. It was true, then, Papa and Aunt Jem received stolen goods and no-one thought any the worse of them. Her new ball gown, too. Yes, she was also involved. So in a way this was good news because she felt now that she could become a real friend to Ned, smuggler although he was.

She smiled through the shadows. 'And what else do you smuggle, I wonder?'

'Tobacco, snuff, rich materials . . .' He was smiling back at her, his voice easy again. 'And sometimes precious stones. But, Miss Charlie . . .'

Shyly she interrupted, 'Don't call me Miss. I'm just Charlie.'

'Thank you.' He touched her hand again, before continuing, 'Well, Charlie, although most local men smuggle a bit and no-one thinks badly of them, there are other men up country who are really wicked, planning wrecks and fights in order to bring much more expensive goods in and so add to their riches. We have to keep our eyes open to be wary of them and their evil plans and make sure we don't get blamed for their wicked work.'

Charlie thought again. 'Wrecks and fights? That sounds horrible. I hope you don't meet any of those wicked men down here.'

'Well, there's always the possibility.' Ned was silent for a moment. 'We have a good network of people watching and listening. Spying, I suppose you would call it. Our local villagers keep an eye open for new people arriving, for new ways being brought in, for anything strange happening . . .'

Although the shadows half hid his face, Charlie read his expression and heard the question in his quiet voice. She said unsteadily, 'Are you suggesting that I am one of those people who should be spying, Ned? I'm a local girl, and I'm interested in everything that goes on in the village, so I suppose . . .'

He drew in a heavy breath. 'Charlie, I'm not suggesting anything, just leaving it up to you to remember as you go about your everyday life, and perhaps, if ever . . .'

'If ever I see or hear anything odd, to tell you?'

He nodded. 'Or Andy Reddaway, or his father, Pete, who is your gardener. These are good people, Charlie, who want to keep the peace in their village. You can trust them with a message if you ever want to send one.'

She found it difficult to accept all he had said. Would a smuggler tell anyone such tales? And then her spirits rose, for this was an adventure which would be much more exciting than dressing up in men's clothing and going sailing with Andy Reddaway. Sending messages to smugglers? And what if Papa found out? She half smiled. He couldn't do anything, could he, not if he continued accepting those kegs of brandy.

'Very well.' Her voice was firm, her smile brighter. Talking to Ned had cleared her mind and now she understood about the local smuggling she wouldn't worry any more. If by chance she ever heard of wicked men arriving, she would certainly pass on the message. Tell Andy or even Mr Reddaway. Her mind sparked. Would Ned himself whistle beneath her window again in the hope of receiving some news?

She stood up and pulled the cloak more closely about her. 'I must go now. It's dangerous for you to be here, someone might easily hear your horse's hooves.'

'I'll make sure we go by a quiet path, Charlie.'

He stood, looking down at her and smiling that handsome smile which quickened her emotions and made her heart beat faster. 'But before you go, I have something for you.' He put a hand to his pocket and took out something which he offered her.

She took it. Something hard and of a curious shape. It took only a few seconds to understand. 'A shell! Oh, Ned, thank you, but what sort is it? I don't think I've ever seen one of these before.'

'It's a conch shell, Charlie. I found it on a beautiful sandy beach thousands of miles from here. A beach where I'd like to take you one day. Where the sun shines and the sea is warm and filled with amazing shells and fish. A place I think you'd like . . .'

Charlie was silent as joy and wonder mingled in a confusion of thoughts. She held the shell carefully and stared up into his eyes. 'You asked me before, didn't you? To sail off with you. But I can't possibly do that.'

He took the hand that held the conch shell and brought it up to her ear. 'Perhaps one day it might be possible. But for now, if you listen to this, you'll hear the waves surging and lilting inside it, and you'll know that wherever I am, on the sea, I'm thinking of you.'

Charlie shut her eyes because the picture he drew was too wonderful, and too impossible to really look at. When she opened them again she felt his hands release hers, leaving the shell warm against her body. Whispering, she said, 'Thank you, Ned, and I shall listen—yes, and think of you.'

He stepped away, out of the summer house, into the growing darkness of the night, and said quietly, 'So it's farewell until we meet again, Charlie. I shall remember being here with you. But for now, good night.'

She stayed where she was, looking out into the still garden imagining him unhitching his horse, mounting and then slowly and carefully riding along rough grass, not making any sound, leaving her alone and suddenly very unhappy.

The shell in her hands was a reminder of what had been a wonderful meeting and she knew she would do just as Ned had said—she would listen to the sea music in the conch, and even dream of seeing that sandy beach, under the foreign sun, that he had conjured up for her.

THE MYSTERY DEEPENS

When Charlie awoke next morning her first thoughts were of Jane. Unhappily, she felt that she had upset her friend by talking about Bradley spending time with her in the grotto—

well, today she would go and find Jane and explain a few things.

As she dressed, she planned what to say. Nothing about Ned, of course, but enough about the decoration of the grotto to interest her, because she had a good idea that Jane could be helpful in keeping Bradley amused while she worked with her shells.

Packing up her shell bag after breakfast, and making sure that the beautiful creamy conch shell was well hidden, she bade goodbye to her aunt and made her way down the hill, stopping as she passed Dr Edwards' house and going through the neat garden to the front door where she knocked and waited.

The elderly maid said Jane was in her little studio, just outside the french windows at the back of the house. 'I'll tell her you're here, Miss Westland . . .' she said, but Charlie shook her head. 'Don't bother, Mary. I know the way. I'll go and find her myself.'

Jane was sitting at her easel just inside the studio, industriously applying her brush to the seascape in front of her. She looked up with a smile. 'Charlie! I mean, Charlotte, how nice to see you . . .' And then, suddenly the smile died and her voice grew tight. 'What are you doing here? I imagined you to be up at The Look Out with Bradley Reed in their old grotto . . .'

Charlie tucked in her skirt, sat down on the ground just inside the door and looked up at her friend with mischievous eyes. 'I do believe you're jealous, Jane Edwards! Whatever has got into you? I told you the other day that I don't much care for Bradley Reed. And that's why I need your help.'

'Oh!' Jane paused, brush in the air and stared down at Charlie. 'So tell me what you mean.'

I mean that I want you to come to The Look Out with me and keep Bradley out of my way in the grotto. You see, he's trying to take over all my work. Couldn't you suggest he shows you around the garden, or takes you to the stables to inspect that big grey horse of his?'

They stared at each other for a long moment, and Charlie saw Jane's smile slowly return. She put down her brush. 'So you don't want him to pay you any attention, as I thought he was doing? But are you sure, Charlie? I mean, he's such a handsome man, so pleasant, so . . .' Jane's voice hushed to a whisper, 'So attractive.'

Charlie looked away, trying to conceal her amusement. 'You're welcome to him, Jane. Please come with me, will you? It will only be for an hour and then you can suggest he drives you home again . . .'

Jane started cleaning her brushes and covering the half-finished canvas. 'Shall we walk to The Look Out? It's not far up the hill and we can look at the sea as we go.'

Such a lovely morning, with the sun glinting on the waves, enhancing the beautiful picture of sky and ocean. The girls paused on the cliff path overlooking the bay and looked out towards the horizon. Then Charlie remembered what Ned had said about the music of the sea. She listened attentively and, yes, she could hear it. Gulls in the distance, waves below the cliff beating against rocks, and the gentle lapping swell of the ocean itself. *Sea music . . .*

Charlie saw that Jane was concentrating on the slow rhythm of the waves as they rolled over the sand below, but she was more interested in the different boats out there, silhouetted against the horizon—small fishing boats from the village, perhaps Andy in the *Daisy Ann*, she wondered—and then saw a bigger one, a schooner, or perhaps what had Andy warned her about, a lugger?

A thrill of excitement ran through her, remembering his words. Until then she had thought smugglers used their own small fishing boats when they were off-loading their goods, but Andy had said the big lugger with three sails was probably used by more dangerous, possibly aimed men, he had said, with a frown.

She was so busy imagining these things that when a voice said brightly, 'Good morning, ladies. Enjoying the view, are you?' She spun around in surprise.

Bradley Reed was mounted on his big grey horse. Smiling down at them, he dismounted and gestured out to sea. 'No doubt what has

78

caught your eye is my boat out there. She's a beauty, isn't she? And, of course, you are both coming out for a sail sometime soon. I think we should make it next week. Would that be convenient for you?' He bowed to Jane and added, 'For both of you?'

Charlie saw that Jane's pale face had grown becomingly pink, her hazel eyes full of smiles and pleasure, and so she kept quiet, allowing her friend to answer for them both.

'Oh, Mr Reed, how exciting. Yes, I'm sure we can come next week.' She half turned. 'Can't we, Charlie?'

Charlie smiled and nodded and Jane went on, 'So which day do you suggest, Mr Reed?'

Bradley looked down at Jane and gave her a returning smile, saying smoothly as he did so, 'Surely you can call me by my christian name, Miss Edwards? I should be delighted if you will do so.'

Jane's colour flamed and she bowed her head. 'Of course, Bradley . . .' Her voice faded and she looked at Charlie as if for help.

'Well,' said Charlie, 'if I have to choose a day next week, I would make it any day except Friday, because the last two Fridays have been rainy, so why don't we make the trip on Thursday?'

Hurriedly she thought that this would give her a good week in which to try and discover more about Ned and his smuggling. Then it struck her, perhaps he would be interested in the elegant boat moored just out in the bay? Not that Bradley was one of those wicked men he spoke of, but even so a new boat on the scene might be important. Could she get a message to him? Andy, she thought, or Mr Reddaway.

'Thursday. Very well, let's make it then. All right with you, Miss Edwards?'

'Jane, if you please . . .' Again Jane's eyes lowered, and at once Bradley smiled.

'Jane, such a pretty name. Thank you. You know, I feel as if we're old friends now.' He paused, then continued, 'and are you accompanying Charlotte on her walk to the Manor, I wonder? How pleasant if you are. Let me escort you and then we'll join my sister in some chocolate in the gazebo before the work on the shells commences.'

Leading his horse, Bradley placed himself on the cliff edge side of the footpath, and they slowly climbed the hill leading up to his home.

Charlie was silent, listening to Jane making easy conversation with Bradley, and wondering all the time how she was right in thinking she must get a message to Ned. It wasn't anything to do with Bradley being a possible smuggler—well, of course he wasn't—but the fact that the big ship was moored so close to the shore that had sent an instinctive warning into her busy mind.

By the time they turned in at The Look Out, she was sure of what she must do. Collect more shells this afternoon, and at the same time climb up through the Devil's Whisper and go down into the village to find Andy. But in the meantime, there must be polite conversation with Miss Felicia over the chocolate

'Good morning. How nice to have visitors.' Miss Felicia was already sitting in the gazebo, which was situated on a high mound at the top of the garden with a good view of the horizon beyond the cliff edge. She put down her embroidery and said, 'Do sit down, young ladies. Bradley, tell the maid to bring chocolate and some ratafia biscuits.' After he had gone, she turned her dark, deep-set eyes on the two girls sitting quietly opposite her, and looked at them very intently. 'And what have you two been doing, I wonder? Where did Bradley find you? Out for a walk, were you? Enjoying the sea view?'

'Yes,' said Jane. 'The waves were quiet this morning, and I was studying their shape and colour so that I can try and capture them in my painting, you see, Miss Reed.'

'Quite so. Sensible of you to study, my dear, and so enhance your talent. And you, Miss Westland? What were you looking at?'

Charlie thought rapidly and then said, 'I was looking at the splendid ship anchored out there just beyond the bar of the harbour, and then your brother came along and said it was his! We were so surprised, and then we talked about having a trip out in her next week.'

'On Thursday,' said Jane, smiling happily.

'Of course. I hope you're both good sailors.' Miss Felicia's voice deepened and Charlie studied her intently. She thought the eyes glittered with sudden interest, and saw the claw-like fingers decorated with those huge rings, clasp one another, and wondered if Miss Felicia approved of her brother's invitation, or not. Then Bradley reappeared, and then the maid with a tray of chocolate and biscuits and conversation reverted to the happy financial outcome of the bazaar sales towards the church funds.

Charlie stole a glance at Jane as she said, 'I hear you are planning a great change in your garden, Bradley. Removing some of the old shrubs and replacing with new plants, I believe. It all sounds so exciting. And Jane is particularly interested in designing gardens, aren't you, Jane?'

'I—what? Oh yes, of course I am. Designing gardens, why, yes, yes.'

Bradley took the bait at once. 'Then Jane, I hope you will allow me to take you around and show you what I plan to do? I shall be very interested to hear your thoughts on the subject.'

'That would be lovely, er, Bradley. Thank you.' Jane sipped her chocolate and avoided Charlie's amused eyes.

When the refreshments were finished, Charlie watched Bradley escort Jane into the garden, and knew she must now go to the grotto and start her work. So she smiled at Miss Felicia, who was picking up her embroidery once more, and said, 'Forgive me for leaving you, Miss Reed, but I must get on with my shell work. Thank you for the pleasant interlude. Goodbye,' and fled before her hostess could reply.

She entered the grotto with mixed feelings. Yes, it was lovely to be on her own, with an hour's work on the shells awaiting her, but something felt strange here in the lantern lit cave. But she soon got down to the work, losing herself in the business of removing broken shells and then replacing them.

She found that Mr Reddaway had left her a big pail of mortar, ready to be used when necessary. He must have done it before the end of the day, and after Bradley had said he need stay no longer. A warm feeling swept through Charlie as she thought about the old gardener and his willingness to help in any way possible.

The time was passing so quickly. Now the rose blossom looked very much better, with its greyish yellow, broken shells replaced with new, gleaming ones, fresh from the beach.

Charlie again found the little hidey-hole beneath the middle shell, and wondered once more who had made it, and what it was for. She took extra care when fixing the replacement shell over the small space, and built the mortar half an inch higher so that the centre shell was slightly uplifted. She might need to find it one day. She smiled to herself, banishing the exciting imaginary thoughts that so often insisted on filling her mind.

It might be nearly time to go, Jane and Bradley would probably appear at any moment. Charlie stepped back, inspecting very carefully the work she had done, and finding it satisfactory. She then caught her breath. There were strange sounds within the grotto—she swiveled around, listening, staring into the darkness, holding the lantern up high. Nothing moved but—there, again—the sounds continued. She remained motionless, eyes wide, fear suddenly twitching through her. What had Mr Reddaway said? Old tales of the sad young woman's ghost . . . of unpleasant things happening . . . and yes, even Papa had mentioned folktales. Cold shivers ran down Charlie's back, and then she sucked in a huge breath. Footsteps, definitely, footsteps were approaching in the distance, coming nearer, not from outside, but from in here, in a distant part of the grotto which was invisible.

She had a momentary desire to run, but then her spirit of adventure, never far away, banished such feebleness. Bravely she told herself that if they were footsteps, then someone was making them. And if she waited that someone would appear . . .

She waited. Footsteps came nearer.

Charlie's blood pounded and she retreated a couple of steps, until her back was against the wall. And then she saw, through the darkness, emerging into the lantern light, a man was pushing his way out of what seemed to be a tunnel.

She held her breath, waited, watched . . . and then saw Andy Reddaway stretch himself upright, standing there brushing dirt and rubbish off his clothes, and then, blinking into the lantern light, suddenly seeing her.

He was grinning. 'Why, Charlie,' he said, 'I was hoping to find you here.'

'Goodness,' said Charlie in surprise, returning his smile. 'How ever did you get here? You didn't come through the entrance, did you?'

'Through the tunnel.' Andy nodded and gestured back over his shoulder. ''Tis a proper business, that, having to bend down and not fall over the stones that lie around, but I made it.'

Charlie's eyes widened. 'The tunnel? What tunnel? What do you mean?'

'Why, there's a narrow tunnel through the cliff into this grotto. Dad found it yesterday when he was bringing a bucket of mortar in for you to use with your shells, and then he, well, sort of explored as far as he could see, and there was this tunnel.'

'But Mr Reed said he wasn't needed any more as no work was to be done in here, apart from the shells on this panel . . .' Charlie was puzzled.

Andy hesitated. 'I know, but Dad's curious, see, and he remembered old tales about a tunnel somewhere. So he stayed on and tried to follow it as far as he could.'

Good old Mr Reddaway. Charlie was delighted. 'But how have you managed to get here now?'

Andy puffed out his chest. 'Sounded exciting, so this mornin' I had a go at finding my way back through it. Found a little cave entrance on the cliff, and dug myself in. I knew you'd be here.'

'How did you know?'

Andy grinned again. 'The whole village knows, that's how! Must have seen you comin' here with your bag of shells, and that was enough.'

'Gossip!' said Charlie crossly, but she couldn't stop herself smiling.

A tunnel—coming out somewhere on the cliff face. Was it for smugglers? Had smugglers always used it and if so, did that have anything to do with the rose flower? What about the hidey hole? Had they used it for something to do with smuggling all those years ago? What was the tale about a jewel being stolen?

Andy was staring at her. 'What you thinking, Charlie? You look all excited.'

'Show me the tunnel! Come on, Andy, quickly, before Mr Reed comes to find me.'

She was at his side, tugging at his arm, and then she heard footsteps and voices, and turned again, pushed Andy away, forcing him back into the darkness. She moved quickly, back to her bag of shells and the beautiful rose panel, just in time to greet Jane, followed by Bradley, as they appeared in the grotto entrance.

'Time for luncheon, I think,' said Bradley cheerily as he came inside and stood beside Jane, watching Charlie hurriedly sorting out her shells. 'Why, Charlotte, what a difference you have made to that flower . . .'

He smiled at her as she nodded her head, wishing all the time that he and Jane would disappear. But she had the sense to answer, 'Thank you, Bradley, and tomorrow I shall do even more.' She gave her friend a marked look, and said firmly, 'Now, Jane, don't tread on my bag of shells—why don't you and Bradley go and organise the trap ready to take us home while I pack up all my bits and pieces? I'll join you very shortly.'

Jane took a few seconds to understand, but then said very rapidly, 'What a good idea. Come along, Bradley—and perhaps we could have a few words with Miss Felicia about the plants I have suggested for the garden?'

They disappeared and at last Charlie felt free to ask Andy, hiding back in the shadows, to take her to the tunnel. 'I'll leave my shells here—take the lamp, Andy, and I'll follow where you go . . . just for a moment . .'

It was a dark and dirty path he took, bending low and warning her not to bang her head against the ceiling. Charlie hitched up her skirt and nodded impatiently. 'All right, just go on and take me through this horrid tunnel —I can't wait to see where it leads.'

Some few minutes later a small circle of light appeared at the end of the narrow tunnel, and Charlie could smell the sea out there, in the sunlight. She pushed Andy ahead of her. 'Hurry up! I want to get some fresh air . . .'

The tunnel ended suddenly in a small cave high up in the cliff overlooking the bay.

Charlie stuck her head out of the entrance and looked down. A narrow, dangerous looking path lead from the cave down the sloping cliff face into the bay itself. She thought of Andy climbing up here and was impressed with his bravery. Then she thought of smugglers in the past, for they must have used this tunnel and the grotto for storing their illegal goods—making the dangerous climb in the dark, and perhaps with a strong wind raging.

She remembered that she wanted Andy to take a message to Ned. 'We'd better go back now or Mr Reed will wonder where I am, but Andy, will you please take a message for me?'

They were making their return journey to the grotto and it was hard to speak as they bent and crawled along, but once back within the stone walls, Charlie dusted dirt off her dress and said urgently, 'Andy, tell Ned, the smuggler, that the Reeds have come to live here recently. And Mr Reed owns the schooner in the bay.'

Andy stared at her. 'But you don't think Mr Reed is involved in . . .?' He bit off the word,

'No, of course not. That's quite ridiculous, but I told Ned I would inform him of anything strange going on in the village, anyone new moving in, so please tell him, will you?'

Andy scratched his head but nodded. 'Yes, I will—next time I see him. He doesn't come into the village very often and tonight, of course, he'll be extra busy . . .'

'Tonight? Why?' Charlie had picked up her bag of shells, and lingered for a last moment in the grotto entrance.

'Dark of the moon tonight. A landing down in the bay, and then loaded horses and carts coming up through the village when everyone's in bed. Make sure you don't leave the house, Charlie.'

Excitement raged through Charlie like a suddenly lit fire, but somehow she managed to keep her voice calm, as she nodded at him, and said, 'Don't worry about me, Andy. I'm quite sensible these days.'

He gave her a long look and grinned. 'I'll believe that when it happens, Charlie. But I've got to go now before anyone sees me here.'

'And so have I. Goodbye, Andy, and don't forget the message.' Charlie ran down the garden and into the courtyard where Jane was already in the trap, with Bradley holding the pony's reins and looking impatiently towards the garden.

'Come along, Charlotte,' he called. 'I thought you must have got lost in the grotto, you've been so long.'

Charlie smiled at him, as she climbed up beside Jane and stowed her bag in the back of the trap. 'Thinking of those ghosts who live there, were you, Bradley? Well, I'm not afraid of anything like that.'

He took his seat, cracked the whip and they drove smartly out of the yard and down the hill towards Headland House, but he turned to Charlie and said very firmly, and without a smile, 'Even so, I think you should only spend a very short time each day in the grotto. It's not at all a healthy place to be. All that dust and dirt . . . no, you should definitely not be there.'

Charlie didn't reply, merely smiled, but then caught Jane's eye which was fixed on a large smear of black dust which showed up on her pale skirt.

'How on earth did you get that?' Jane asked, but Charlie shook her head and glared at her. Really, everyone was being most difficult; Bradley trying to stop her going to the grotto and now Jane telling tales about her getting

90

dirty. She dismounted from the trap as it halted at the stable door at Headland House, and waved her hand, calling, 'Goodbye, see you tomorrow morning,' before entering the kitchen and going straight up to her room to change and clean herself before Aunt Jem's eagle eye detected something not quite right.

In the afternoon she paid her usual visit to the bay, her shell bag in evidence, and a knot of excitement in her stomach.

If Andy was right, and the smugglers were off-loading a cargo of contraband tonight, she wished she could be there, but she knew it was impossible. She had given her word to Papa not to slip away in disguise any more. She looked around the empty bay and wished she could somehow get involved with the smugglers. With her bag of shells hidden behind a scrubby plant on the edge of the bay, she climbed up into the huge, dark cave, her blood starting to race.

The tide was turning, small waves already running up the sandy beach into the entrance of the cave, their music singing in her ears. By tonight it would be high tide, just right for a small boat to slip into the darkness, and off-load all the cargo on to the waiting horses and carts that would be up there at the top of the cliff. They would hide them somewhere, of course, and then in the days ahead carefully deliver them to their customers. She frowned. The vicar, Aunt Jem, Papa?

While she was thinking all this, sitting on a rock and watching the waves creep an inch at a time into the cave mouth, she suddenly saw a man entering the cave, his legs bare, striding through the lace topped waves. It was Ned. She got to her feet hurriedly, not sure whether to run or to stay.

Then a familiar voice called out, 'Charlie! What are you doing, here?' and she smiled a welcome. He splashed through the water and approached the rock on which she stood. 'Another adventure, Charlie?'

She felt herself blush, but her voice was steady. 'I—' and then felt her feet slip beneath her on a strand of green seaweed. 'Oh!'

He was beside her in a few strides, strong arms catching her as she lost balance, feeling herself falling from the rock. 'I've got you—steady, now . . .' His voice was reassuring, his hands holding her strong and secure, supporting her as she regained her balance, but the damage was done. She had felt the warmth of his body, seen the sudden light in his sea-green eyes and knew herself hopelessly lost in his charm and strength. For a moment—longer, thought Charlie ecstatically—they stayed together, looking at each other, until she caught a deep breath and knew she must stay no longer.

Reluctantly she pulled away from his arms and stood straight at his side. 'That was so silly of me. I didn't see the weed.'

He raised one dark eyebrow in amusement and said 'A good thing I was here to catch you.'

'Yes.'

His lips moved in a swift, brief grin. 'I had an idea you would be here, on yet another adventure. Am I right, Charlie?'

'You mean you got my message? You've seen Andy?' In a way it was a blessing to get back to ordinary conversation after that wonderful shared moment.

'I have and he told me about the Reeds moving into the village, and about the schooner out there in the bay, but, Charlie . . .' Ned's eyes were suddenly darker, his face taut and he reached forward urgently to take her hand. 'Tonight another boat will be moored here—a lugger bearing contraband, so if you hear any noises.'

She gasped. 'Horse hooves? Voices? Cart wheels?'

He nodded. 'All of those. Just don't take any notice. And the lugger will be gone before dawn, with the ebbing tide. So you don't have to worry about anything.'

'And you, Ned? Where will you be?' She could see it all in her mind, the small rowing boat carrying goods from the big ship, the men using the high tide to bring the boat right into this cave, and then the journey up the dangerous, narrow cliff path to the waiting carts and horses. Adventure, yes, but one thing worried her. Would Ned be one of those men rowing the boat, off-loading kegs of brandy, packets of laces and tobacco, and goodness knows what other rare goods?

He frowned. 'Don't think about me, Charlie. I told you when we first met that all I could tell you was my name for the moment. Well, that still holds.' His eyes caught hers in a dark shadowed gaze and she shivered at his suddenly hard expression.

'But, but,' She ran out of words. How could she possibly tell him what she felt for him? How she longed, with all her heart, to know exactly what he was, who he was—and whether she would ever see him again.

Out of the blue something deep inside her made unexpected words erupt. 'Please take care, Ned. I don't know what you're doing, but it sounds very dangerous, whatever it is, and I'm afraid in case something goes wrong.'

His eyes were very deep and his hands reached out for hers. 'Charlie, you mustn't feel like that. I never meant you to get involved in what I am doing, so just try and forget everything I've said.'

'But I can't possibly do that, Ned.' Her voice trembled. 'Because you've said some lovely things to me, and, well, I thought you meant them . . .'

For a long moment he searched her face and then his own expression darkened. 'Well, I'm asking you now, Charlie, to forget it all, yes, everything I've said. I never wanted to bring you into all this. Please forgive me.' He looked around. 'The tide's coming in fast and I'll take you back to the beach.'

His arms were strong and reassuring and at once she was being swung forward and carried out of the cave through the increasingly fast rolling waves, into the surf, where she saw a small rowing boat bobbing at anchor.

She was too shocked to say anything more but watched his face as he rowed. Grounding the boat on the beach, he looked at her, smiled warmly and his voice was quiet. 'Try and forget me, Charlie. You see, I must keep you safe.'

She had no reply, but watched him take the boat out again into the waves, and slowly row away, out of sight. Then, tearful and with a heavy heart, she went and found the hidden shell bag, and slowly walked home. As she went, she thought of the poor girl in the grotto who had, like her, been unlucky in love. But at least the girl had the token of a sculptured rose to remember her lover by, and perhaps a small jewel, hidden in the heart of the flower . . .

And then Charlie remembered the conch shell Ned had given her, and as she found it in its hiding place, and held it in her hands, listening to the sea music, very slowly her spirits lifted. For, of course, like the poor girl in the grotto, she could never forget the man she knew she loved.

A SHOCKING DISCOVERY

Retreating to her bed early and remembering all that had happened—all that had been felt and said this afternoon in the cave with Ned—Charlie lay dreaming.

Then the rosy dreams faded and she thought about the smuggling taking place, probably at this very moment, quite close to the house. The promise to Papa must be forgotten, for it was vital that she knew if Ned was safe. Surely Papa would forgive such a lapse, if he knew about her feelings?

Something told her she must find out if Ned really was one of the smugglers taking such terrible risks as they carried the illegal goods up the cliff path, and into safe places for storage before the goods were finally taken to their new homes throughout the village.

She got up, thought hard for a moment or two, and then, instead of putting on the disguise, hidden so well in the bottom of the wardrobe, compromised with a dark cloak over a plain warm day dress, and sensible winter shoes.

It was easy to slip out of the still house, treading quietly down the path, letting herself out of the gate and on to the cliff path. Beneath her she heard sea music, but so different this time. Waves were rolling and pounding against the rocks, their rhythm no longer gentle and enjoyable, but strong and threatening.

She thought she heard voices, and went on more rapidly. A wind had risen, and her hair was blowing about, but she pulled the hood of the cloak over her head and ran on, heading for the tiny, hidden path leading to the Devil's Whisper. She heard the full tide booming furiously in the cave, felt spray in the wild wind and tasted salt on her lips.

Suddenly she realised that, on the cliff path ahead of her, horses stood fidgeting, with men holding their reins and other figures appearing out of the darkness of the cave, carrying kegs and packets. She caught her breath, stepped back into what little shelter she could find, and tried desperately to make out the features of the men emerging on the cliff path.

No moonlight tonight, of course—so she had to rely on what she could hear in the voices that the wind blew around her. Someone giving orders—a deep, authoritative voice; and someone else saying quite clearly, 'But it's a dangerous path, sir,' and then the quick, stern order, 'Get on with the work or else it'll be the worse for you, Ben Luscombe.'

Crouching in the undergrowth, she heard murmurs of complaint, but then the figures carrying all the packages began disappearing, clearly doing as they were bid and following a different path. Charlie waited until silence reigned again and knew that all the goods were now being carried to a secret hideaway.

She hadn't heard Ned's voice, or seen anyone looking like him, but of course it was very dark and she supposed that he could have been any one of those many labouring figures—and who was the man with the stern voice? Not Ned. She sighed with relief.

Now she was cold, chilled to the bone, and wanting only to get home safely and without anyone seeing her. It was a rough path leading back to the house, but she made it without accident and soon was in her bedroom again, removing the heavy dark clothes and slipping into bed, where almost at once, she fell into an exhausted sleep. No dreams troubled her, and in the morning, when she awoke, it was with a feeling of immediate relief Ned hadn't been one of the smugglers.

* * *

Next day Jane was waiting for her in the lane outside the house when Charlie left for The Look Out with her bag of shells. After greeting each other, they walked in silence along the cliff path, until Charlie could keep quiet no longer. 'Jane,' she said cautiously, 'there were smugglers here last night. The big lugger was moored in the bay, and all the goods.'

Jane frowned. 'Goods? What goods?'

'Contraband—tobacco, snuff, brandy.'

Charlie hesitated, then added, 'Your father enjoys brandy, doesn't he? Well, where does he get it from, I wonder?'

Jane stopped in midstep, staring at her. 'Oh, no! Father would never deal with anything smuggled. I mean, I don't think he would, but then, those bottles in the cellar . . . and I don't know who delivered them. Oh, Charlie, you don't really think, do you?'

'Probably, Jane, but don't be upset. Apparently the whole village deals in smuggled goods. Why, I expect that even my new ballgown is made of muslin that comes from abroad with no duty paid.'

'How do you know? Who told you all this? Oh, Charlie, you haven't been off on one of your adventures again, have you?'

Charlie laughed at the expression of horror on her friend's face. 'I shan't tell you, Jane, because it's best that you don't know. But, oh Jane, I think I'm in love.'

'Not with a smuggler, I hope?'

Charlie sighed deeply. 'I don't know who he is. Except that he's called Ned.'

'But you can't possibly love someone without a proper name. And where did you meet him?'

By now Charlie was confused and wished she could tell Jane the whole story of Ned, the smugglers last night, and the sad tale of the rose in the grotto. She stopped and faced her friend.

'Let's sit down for five minutes, Jane. I have a lot to tell you . . .'

It didn't take long and at the end of the story Jane had recovered from her shock and was listening intently. 'Smugglers! The way you speak of them they sound really romantic. What a picture they would make, rowing the boat into the cave, and then carrying the goods up the horrible little path. Oh, Charlie, I think I could really paint that picture, you know!'

'I'm sure you could, Jane. And perhaps it might even help to sell all your other pictures.'

Jane got to her feet, looking very serious. 'Do you know, Charlie, I think perhaps I shall try and do that. How I wish I could go to London and study art there.'

Charlie smiled. 'And leave Bradley Reed behind you?'

'Oh!' said Jane, blushing suddenly. 'I hadn't thought of that.'

They continued along the path, with the sea and its music far below the cliff edge, eventually reaching The Look Out, where Jane went indoors to talk to Miss Felicia, and Charlie at once went towards the grotto. She put down her bag of shells and looked at the rose panel, seeing that the work she had already done was creamy and glowing, showing up the other dirty shells, and she started sorting out replacements for them.

A bucket of mortar had been left just inside the entrance and she knew Mr Reddaway had been back again, getting it ready for her. That brought her thoughts back to last night's smuggling run, and she wondered just how involved he and Andy were. But then the work took over, and she began thinking back to the sad story of the girl who had loved the man who created the beautiful flower she was working on.

If only she knew more about the girl, then she thought of old Mrs Endacott—surely she would know something about the old story? Yes, she would go and visit the farm this afternoon.

Half way through her allotted time in the grotto she heard footsteps and voices and Jane and Bradley appeared, coming through the entrance and standing by the lantern, looking at her work. 'You've made it all look quite new,' said Jane admiringly. 'How clever you are, Charlie.'

'Charlie?' Bradley's voice was deep, and something in Charlie's memory stirred. But she smiled at him over her shoulder.

'You know me as Charlotte. It's my proper name, you see.'

'But Charlie is a boy's name . . .' He sounded shocked.

Jane at once said, 'Charlie has always been a tomboy. She loves adventures, you see, and that's why she calls herself by the boy's name.'

'Adventures?' Bradley asked slowly, and looking at him, Charlie saw his dark eyes narrow. She looked quickly at Jane and shook her head. This conversation was going all the wrong way, she thought.

Jane came to her aid at once. 'Oh, harmless little ones, Bradley—nothing very serious. Nowadays she's a proper young lady, like me, thinking of social calls and—and, parties, and balls.' She paused for a second and then added, with a blush, 'and of course, the trip we're both looking forward to in your schooner next week.'

'Ah yes,' said Bradley in a warmer voice and with an approving smile at both girls.

'Thursday it is. I am so looking forward to having you on board. But before that, my sister would like to invite you and your families to dinner one night. We think it's high time we got to know our near neighbours in the village. She will be sending notes around to you—so please keep the next few evenings free, won't you?'

Charlie and Jane exchanged glances and then both smiled and said, 'Thank you, how nice. We shall be delighted to accept the invitation.'

'Good. But now it's high time you came out of this gloomy old grotto, Charlotte—and Jane, I'm hoping you will be able to advise me about some problems in the exotic garden at the end of the lawn. Charlotte, please pack up your shells and come with us . . .'

But Charlie had other ideas, one in

particular. She said quickly, 'It'll take me a few minutes, Bradley, to finish this small part of the panel, so I'll come and join you as soon as it's finished. Don't bother to wait for me.'

She thought Bradley's face tightened as he looked at her, but he merely said, 'Very well. Don't be long, will you? Come along then, Jane.' And they both left the grotto.

As soon as she heard no more footsteps and voices, Charlie left the shell work, picked up the lantern, holding it above her head, and went at once into the darkness, towards the tunnel which she knew led down into the bay. Last night's adventure had led her to think that this particular offloading of goods had been stored up here—a dangerous path, Ben Luscombe had said, and then had been told to 'get on with it.'

Suddenly she stopped and stood quite still. The deep authoritative voice was one she knew. When Bradley Reed ordered his servants, this was the way it sounded. So he had been there last night! Her heart was racing and she blinked several times to focus on the memories of what she had seen there in the Devil's Whisper. *Bradley was a smuggler!* Her thoughts flew then to Ned. Two men, pretending to be someone else . . . why, it was surely impossible!

But then she thought of the goods being unloaded, and knew that facts couldn't be argued with. And that brought her back to the idea of searching the tunnel for the goods which she was sure had been stored here last night.

She stepped slowly forward, lantern held high above her head. Signs in the dirty, stony floor as if boots had been treading up and down, but no trace of any kegs or packets. She wondered if Bradley, or one of his servants, had been up early, organising the removal of the smuggled goods, before she arrived at the grotto. That must be the case, she thought. And then, just as she was about to turn and retrace her steps, knowing that he would be expecting to see her in the garden very soon, something stopped her. She was treading on what felt like a big pebble. In the darkness she bent, and allowed the lantern to show her what was there beside her shoe.

It was a small packet, well wrapped, and of a size that could have been easily kicked aside and forgotten when the other, larger goods, were retrieved. Charlie felt excitement race through her as she picked it up, allowed her fingers to feel around its circular shape and the smoothness of the oiled material which wrapped it.

She returned to the centre of the grotto where her shell bag awaited her and at once secreted the small package in the middle of the surrounding shells. Like the conch Ned had given her, this must remain a secret, only to be revealed when she got home, in the safety of her own room.

Smiling to herself, thoughts busily trying to fit together the pieces of the extraordinary jigsaw, she walked down the garden, past the gazebo where Miss Felicia looked up from her embroidery and nodded her head and on, around the pond and into the exotic part of the wilderness where she could just see Jane and Bradley standing and discussing a rather sad-looking tree which clearly did not appreciate having been transported from its sunny and warm home to a cold, wet land where there was always salt in the air.

Suddenly, her thoughts flew to Ned telling her about the magical white sandy beach—and she smiled. She knew how the poor tree was feeling.

*   *   *

It seemed to Charlie that Bradley looked at her now with a strange expression on his handsome face—as if, she thought, he was trying to make out just how much she knew about his smuggling activities. Or, her mind wavered, was she quite wrong in thinking she had recognised his voice? Sounds at night, and in a high wind with other wild noises masking them, could easily be deceptive. But she decided to watch and wait. If he really was a smuggler, then no doubt sooner or later he would show his true colours.

But at the moment he was polite, friendly and charming, which made her wonder even more if she was mistaken. 'May I drive you home, Charlotte?' His smile was wide. 'Or am I to call you Charlie from now on? And if so, perhaps I may hear about some of your so-called adventures?'

No, he mustn't know about her trips out in Andy's boat, or, especially, that dangerous walk along the cliff path last night . . . But he was being very friendly. She glanced at Jane and thought she saw a sign of an expression of annoyance, and reminded herself then that her friend was very caught by Bradley's undoubted charm. So it would be wiser to refuse his offer of a drive, and walk home by herself. She met his enquiring gaze. 'Thank you, but no, I should enjoy the walk. But perhaps Jane would like . . .'

Definitely a quick slide of annoyance on his good-looking face, masked at once, as he nodded. 'Of course. I should be delighted to take her.'

Jane smiled happily, and they all walked back through the garden, into the stable yard, where Bradley disappeared for a moment, finding the groom, and so giving Charlie a chance to talk to Jane quietly 'Don't tell him anything about smuggling. Just remember to talk about other things—our trip on the boat, or the dinner he's inviting us to—can't tell you why, but it's important. Do you understand?'

Jane nodded, but was clearly more interested in sitting close to Bradley as he helped her into the trap. Charlie watched them drive out of the stable yard and into the road and then she made her own way home.

The package she had found in the grotto burned a hole in her bag of shells, and she couldn't wait to be alone so that she could open it. What it might contain she couldn't imagine, but clearly something small and round.

At luncheon Aunt Jem said that she and Charlie's papa had received a hand-delivered note this morning, inviting the family to dinner tomorrow night at The Look Out. 'Your father is in court in town today but I have no doubt that he will accept the invitation. He seems to have taken a liking to young Mr Reed, who he says has excellent manners and equally excellent prospects.' Aunt Jem looked at Charlie with such a meaningful expression that Charlie gasped.

'Oh dear! I know just what you mean, Aunt, but please don't encourage Papa in his ideas about Bradley. You see, I have no intention, no, really, none at all, of having any serious thoughts about him. In fact, I quite dislike him . . .'

Aunt Jem put her knife and fork on her empty plate and said firmly, 'Just remember, Charlotte, that it's not your place to argue with your dear father. If he considers Mr Reed to be a likely suitor, and I believe he does, then you must do all you can to further the friendship. And now, what are you planning to do this afternoon? Not more shells from the beach, surely?'

Charlie choked over the last mouthful of braised veal, but said quickly, 'No, Aunt. I am going to call on Mrs Endacott. She, er,' She tried to think of a likely excuse, and then finished, 'I would like to know the amount my shell arrangements gained in benefitting the church funds and she will tell me. It would perhaps inspire me to do more of them.'

Aunt Jem nodded. 'Very well. And give Mrs Endacott my regards. The clotted cream she sent us last week was very good indeed. Perhaps you might bring another bowl away with you when you leave, for the strawberries are ripening well in this sunshine.'

'Yes,' said Charlie, relieved and when luncheon was finished, went up to her room with a leap of excitement inside her. Now, perhaps, she could open the small package and see what it contained.

Sitting on her bed, the door firmly closed, and knowing that Aunt Jem was having her usual after-luncheon nap, Charlie took the little package from her bag of shells and carefully opened it. Well wrapped in oiled canvas, it yielded slowly to her impatient fingers but at last the final bit of ragging fell away and she was left with a small, round thing in her hand which she stared at wonderingly.

A pearl. A shell so beautiful and delicate that she just sat there, looking at it. Carefully, she moved it around in her hand, at the same time dredging through her mind for information about the finding of such a rare and lovely thing.

Pearls came from oysters in rivers and seas, she knew that, but the most sought after were sea pearls. She had read that divers had to go down to great depths to find them and they were more often found in foreign oceans than in the cold seas around Great Britain. So had some foreign diver held his breath long enough to descend to the sea bed, find this particular oyster and bring it to the surface, where his knife would open the shell and find this small, creamy pearl? She admired it, glowing in the sunlight falling on her hand through the open window.

Charlie took a long breath, thinking of the intrepid diver, and wondered again at the connection with warm seas and sandy beaches. Ned's words echoed in her mind, and suddenly she had a feeling that this pearl might hold some sort of message. If so, what could it be?

Very slowly, she wrapped it once again in the enfolding rags and canvas and placed it back in the middle of the shell bag. It would be safe there—at least until, somehow, she discovered where it came from—and also found out where it should go. Leaving the bag at the bottom of her wardrobe, hidden beneath some heaped shawls, she put on her bonnet, left her room, and began the short walk to Mrs Endacott's farm, further down the hill.

As she walked, she looked at the sea and saw Bradley's schooner moored out in the bay. But there was no sign of the three-sailed lugger that had been anchored here last night.

The mystery was deepening and she frowned as she walked. How could she possibly find the answers to all these strange and seemingly unanswerable questions? It came to her that perhaps Ned might be able to do so, although he was part of the puzzle, too, but how could she get in touch with him? And, alas, he had said she must forget him . . . Charlie's frown slipped into unhappiness, and she was thankful to reach the farm and let Mrs Endacott persuade her to come and sit in the sun and have a nice drink of milk, fresh from the farm cow this morning.

'My dear soul,' said Mrs Endacott in her warm, Devon voice, 'but you look proper peaky—not like the pretty young lady I'm used to seeing. What is it then?'

Charlie sat on the hard wooden bench just outside the kitchen door, overlooking the pig sty, the stables and the cow shed, with hens foraging and clucking around her feet, and at once felt a lot better. She smiled at the elderly woman beside her. 'Mrs Endacott, I have a lot on my mind, and I want to ask if you can help

110

me to clear up a few things.'

'Ask away, my dear, and I'll do what I can.' Her companion's smile was genuine and warm as she refilled Charlie's glass.

'Well . . .' Slowly, sometimes pausing for the right words, Charlie told her about the grotto and the beautiful shell sculpture of the rose. She said she had heard tales about a young lady who lived in the Manor many years ago and did Mrs Endacott know?

'Why yes, that were Miss Rosina Hartley, a lovely girl whose parents stopped her from marrying the artist who did the carving in the grotto. Oh, such a long time ago. And some foolish folks say she's still there, waiting for him to come back, or some such rubbish . . .'

Charlie pondered. Then she said slowly, 'She may not be there, Mrs Endacott, but did she leave something behind her, in the grotto? You see, I've discovered a little hole in the centre of the rose which could have held something small. A ring, perhaps?'

The old woman's expression slid away into memory. 'Could be. Yes, there were things said about treasure, perhaps a ring, or a jewel of sorts, being in the grotto somewhere. Mind you, thieves got in there, no doubt.' She smiled excitedly 'But you've found it, have you, my dear?'

'Well, not exactly,' Charlie said carefully. 'But I have found a pearl, I think it might have been smuggled and left there by accident when

111

the goods were all cleared away this morning . . .'

'Ah, last night, eh?' Mrs Endacott's face grew taut. 'So you know about last night?'

'Yes,' said Charlie. 'I know the lugger brought goods ashore, and that these are different smugglers from the ones we usually have coming into the bay.'

'Indeed they are. Bad men, these, not our usual friendly boys.'

'But, Mrs Endacott, what am I to do with this pearl? Should I give it to someone? The Customs men, for instance?'

'Oh no! Hide it, my dear. Keep it safe. I expect someone will be looking for it soon, and then you'll know a bit more about it all, and what to do. Well, now . . .' Mrs Endacott changed the subject. 'Some more milk, Miss Weston? And perhaps another dish of cream for you to take home?'

Charlie realised that she had been given all the information possible, so she asked about the donation Bradley Reed had made to the church funds when buying her shell arrangement, and was astonished at the small amount he had thought it was worth. Another reason for disliking the man, she thought, as she got up, took the offered dish of cream and made her way home to Headland House.

But she knew Mrs Endacott's advice was good, she must hide the pearl in a safe place so that whoever wanted it would never find it, and perhaps in searching might give himself away. She was trying to think of a good hiding place.

Walking high above the whispering sea, the answer came. She would slip it in behind the centre of the shell rose, in the little hole which someone, Rosina, had made there so many years ago. It would be safe, for no-one knew the hole was there except people whom she could trust—Jane, Mr Reddaway and possibly Andy. Hide the smuggled pearl and then watch to see if anyone came looking for it. Would it be Bradley? Her smile faded. But definitely not Ned.

At home it was teatime and then Papa returned from his day in court so the invitation to the Reeds' dinner party had to be discussed. 'I see no reason why we should not go,' said Aunt Jem, smiling, and looking at Charlie in a meaningful way. 'And, if we do, child, you must wear that pretty new gown, the one with the low top and the big sleeves. You will look very, well, attractive—in that.'

Charlie pursed her lips, knowing exactly what her aunt meant. That Bradley would be even further engaged with her appearance in a revealing dress. 'I don't think—' she started, but Papa interrupted.

'Certainly we'll go,' he said briskly. 'I'll send Eddie around with a note of acceptance. I should very much like to see the Reeds in their own home, for one always gets a much truer idea of character and style of living, I think. So yes, Charlotte, dress yourself up for once.' His smile was warm, with a touch of amusement, as he added, 'not the breeches and boots tomorrow evening, if you please, but something feminine and lovely so that Mr Reed can admire your appearance.'

Charlie said nothing, merely lowered her head in acceptance, but inside she raged.

It seemed that Papa and Aunt Jem were already seeing her as Bradley's bride. The thought was an excruciating one, and after dinner she ran upstairs into her bedroom to sit on her bed and think over everything that had happened today.

She took the pearl out of the shell bag again and held it in her hand, It was warm and beautiful and the moonlight peeping through her open window gave it a special beauty.

Charlie sat looking at it for a long while, thinking over what Mrs Endacott had told her, and wishing that, in some extraordinary way, she could help poor Rosina to rest, instead of haunting the grotto as she was said to do. Could the pearl, smuggled although it undoubtedly was, be a means of laying the little ghost?

But no idea came into her busy mind, and when she lay down to sleep, she dreamed, not of Rosina, but of Ned and a long, scalloped sandy beach, somewhere far away across the ocean, where the sun always shone, and he and

114

she were together.

In the morning she awoke smiling, but then the thoughts of the day ahead of her—and particularly the evening dinner with Bradley and Miss Felicia, put a new expression on her face. She sat up, knowing that somehow today she must take the pearl to the grotto and hide it, and without anyone seeing her do so.

TRUE COLOURS

Later that morning, Charlie was, as usual, joined by Jane on the way to The Look Out, and, as they walked, Charlie told her friend of the remarkable find, a beautiful and probably expensive pearl, left by the smugglers when they stored their contraband in the grotto tunnel.

'I didn't know there was a tunnel . . .'

Charlie sighed. How could Jane be so naïve? 'How do you think I got such dirty marks on my dress, then, if I hadn't been exploring it the other day?'

'Oh!' Jane's face was shocked, and then slowly began to smile. 'Charlie, do tell me more. I mean, I want to put everything into my new picture about smuggling. A cave right at the top of a cliff? With men climbing up with their barrels and packets and then going into it to hide everything. Goodness, what a picture it will make . . .'

Charlie laughed. 'Just wait until we make our trip in Bradley's boat in a few days' time—you'll have all the material you want then.'

'I can't wait. But oh dear, I do hope the sea will be calm.'

Having reached The Look Out, Jane disappeared in search of Bradley, hoping to spend time with him in the wild garden, and Charlie made her way to the grotto. She looked at the rose with new eyes now, seeing in it a secret she had never imagined before.

It was simple to take the pearl out of its hiding place in her bag, to unwrap it, then open up the small centre of the rose and place the pearl inside it. She wished, for a moment, that the jewel could stay there, but of course it was contraband and must eventually be returned to its owner.

Just as she was replacing the mortar and making sure it was completely hidden beneath fresh shells, she heard someone entering the grotto and turned quickly, thinking it must be Bradley. No, it was Miss Felicia, looking about her and then saying, in her deep voice, 'I believe Bradley dropped something in here the other day, Miss Weston. I am just having a look for it . . .'

'Really, Miss Felicia—what was it?'

'Some small article he was bringing home to show me. Probably something he found in the garden. An interesting stone, I believe.'

'Let me help you look.' Charlie took the lantern and held it closer to the floor at Miss Felicia's feet. 'Well, I can't see anything here . . .'

'No. He must have imagined dropping it in here.' Miss Felicia's voice held an edge, and Charlie wondered how brother and sister got on.

But then she heard Jane's voice and Bradley answering her, and lifted the lantern again to focus on the shell work. Miss Felicia stood in the entrance to the grotto, awaiting them, and as they drew nearer, she called to her brother. 'You were wrong, Bradley, there is no sign of anything dropped here. You must look in other places.'

Charlie looked at the three people standing just beyond the entrance. She saw Jane looking wide eyed and puzzled, and gave her a quick smile. But then she was caught by the looks exchanged between Bradley and his sister. No smiles, but frowns and gleaming, narrowed eyes that held annoyance and something stronger, she thought. Something unpleasant.

Bradley pursed his lips, stared at his sister for a long moment and then said harshly, 'I have better things to do, Felicia, than wander around the garden looking for something that probably isn't there. It was only your interest in stones, after all, that made me want to show you this one.'

Conversation was flowing when Charlie

slipped into the gazebo, and sat on the chair Bradley pulled out for her. Jane was asking Bradley something about the rare tulip tree which he planned to put in the garden, but then Miss Felicia interrupted, saying, loudly in her strange voice, 'Never mind about the garden, I understand you young ladies, and your families, will be joining us for dinner this evening. I'm so glad. It's high time Bradley and I expanded our small circle of acquaintances and both your families, Jane and you, Charlotte, will, I'm sure, be able to speak well of us when living their busy lives among the village community. After all,' she smiled, a stiff and what Charlie thought was a hopeful smile, before adding, 'we know only too well that very often uneducated villagers are quick to think ugly thoughts.'

Charlie smiled back at the small woman, who seemed to be watching her very intently, and again noticed the huge rings on her tiny, misshapen fingers. A sapphire, blazing in the sunlight. Something green and dull—could it be jade?' And that blood red stone, as big as Miss Felicia's arthritic knuckles—a cornelian, perhaps.

Then Bradley was speaking, and the image faded as she concentrated on his words.

'Yes, indeed. Dinner tonight, and the sea trip on Thursday!'

She thought he sounded friendly, his cold expression gone, and was pleased that he looked at Jane with a big smile. 'And you, Miss Jane, are you planning to bring a sketch book and make a few drawings ready for your next beautiful picture?'

Jane put her cup back on its saucer and said quickly, with a big smile, 'Oh, yes, Bradley, I most certainly am. But it's not going to be quite the picture you imagine, I think. Not so much another seascape, as something more lively.'

Back in the grotto, Charlie felt that something had been fixed into the puzzle. She wasn't quite sure what, but she knew now very plainly that the Reeds wished to be popular in the village for some reason known best to themselves. Indeed, they thought it was necessary to be so. But why?

The question stayed in her mind, food for thought, as after a while she packed up and walked home, waving to Bradley and Jane trotting past in the trap.

The afternoon was very warm and Charlie looked out of her window down into the bay which, at low tide, was a stretch of sunlit, golden sand. There must be some interesting shells left in the seaweed-littered tide line, but she knew she couldn't go down there today for Aunt Jem had said at luncheon that the afternoon must be spent in making sure that her best gown was uncreased and ready to be worn this evening.

There was a tap on the door and Aunt

Jem came in, offering a length of beautiful pale green velvet ribbon. 'I think it will match your gown very well, and show off your lovely chestnut hair, Charlotte.' She put the ribbon on the dressing table. 'But where is your gown? And I expect your slippers need attention . . . don't waste time, dear child, for before you know it the carriage will be ready to take us to The Look Out.'

It was, in fact, a good three and a half hours before the allotted time for departure, during which Charlotte sat on her bed, dreamed the usual dreams, and then, guilt ridden, got up and found her green taffeta gown. Yes, it was creased. She must ask Susie to iron it for her. And then the silk pumps—oh dear, some stains on them—another job for Susie, but of course she would offer to help . . .

Between hours in the hot kitchen, heating up the flat iron on the range, and then trying to remove stains from the slippers, Charlie chatted to Susie who worked with a will, and was easily persuaded to tell of any village gossip which she thought might amuse her young mistress.

'Well, Miss Charlotte, my ma don't think much of the newcomers at The Look Out. She goes there every day to collect the washing, you see. Miss Felicia's hard on her servants and he—Mr Bradley—always seems to be arguing with the lady.

'Your gown is really lovely now. I'll take

120

it up to your room and hang it. Don't want it creasing again, do us?'

As Charlie dressed, ready for the evening ahead of her, she thought over what Susie had said and wondered, yet again, what all the arguments in the Reeds' home were about. Then Aunt Jem was knocking at the door. 'Are you ready, Charlotte? Your father says the carriage is outside and waiting for us. Let me see how you look, child.'

Charlie stood quietly beneath her aunt's assessing eyes and hoped that the last stain on the left slipper—it had been impossible to remove it—wouldn't show beneath the flounced hem of the green gown. She had looked at herself in the long mirror, and knew that the fashion of very low neck and huge puffed sleeves suited her, with its tiny waist line and many gored skirt, ending in silk frills and embroidered flowers. She hoped Aunt Jem would approve.

Her aunt sighed. 'Charming, my dear, quite charming, and yes, the velvet ribbon with those few flowers entwined in it is just right in your hair. You look very pretty, indeed.' She smiled and then added, 'And I'm sure Mr Bradley will think so, too. Now, Charlotte, do behave this evening. Try to be as nice as you can to him, won't you? Remember what your father expects of you.'

As she followed her aunt down the stairs through the hallway and into the waiting

121

carriage, she felt all her dreams of sailing away to a foreign beach where the shell-laden sand was silvery white and the waves sang sweet music, fall away. Papa had his own dreams for her, and she knew, that, despite her reluctance, as a dutiful daughter she must do as he asked of her.

Sitting in the carriage next to Aunt Jem and facing Papa, she tried to smile and forget all about a certain smuggler who offered all the charm that Bradley Reed was so clearly missing.

* * *

They were greeted warmly at The Look Out, Bradley himself coming into the large hall and conducting them into the drawing-room where Miss Felicia waited.

While greetings were being exchanged, Charlie looked around her, thoughts suddenly switching to the idea of perhaps having to marry Bradley and so become mistress of this ancient house.

But then voices around her caught her interest, and she looked at the group of people standing beside Miss Felicia and talking so busily. Dr Edwards and his wife, and Jane, who smiled at her and raised an eyebrow as if they were still sharing secrets; Mr Harvey Jackson, Papa's friend who was an usher at court; her own papa and Aunt Jemima, chatting to

Miss Felicia and Bradley as if they were close friends.

And then—someone was being shown into the room, giving his hat to the maid servant, and then advancing, looking straight at her—Ned. How extraordinary! What could he be doing here? But she had no time to think further, for Bradley at once left the group he was part of and walked up to the newcomer. He smiled, bowed, gestured him to join the rest of the party, and began introducing him to everybody.

Charlie watched, not believing her own eyes. Ned wore a very handsome navy blue coat with golden trimmings; pristine white trousers, his hair was tidily caught back in a queue tied with a black bow, and he carried white gloves. When Bradley brought him to her side she could only stare. Bradley's voice was full of what she thought was satisfaction. 'May I introduce Miss Charlotte Westland?' he said, smiling. 'Charlotte, this is Lieutenant Ned Drake, the new chief Preventive Officer, recently sent here to rid us of these wicked smugglers.'

Ned bowed, allowed his smile to briefly flower, and then assumed his previous stern expression. 'Miss Westland, it is a privilege to meet you.'

What could she say? How could she keep the surprise out of her eyes as she responded to his smile? 'And it is my pleasure to meet *you*, Mr Drake.'

Bradley was watching them; she saw his smile slip into amusement and wondered why. What was so odd about her meeting Ned here? Unless, of course Bradley knew about her adventures and the trips away from Headland House, and was perhaps trying to trap her into confession. Charlie lifted her head half an inch higher than usual and looked Bradley straight in the eyes. 'So when we were driving along the cliff path the other day,' she said briskly, 'it must have been Mr Drake whom we saw. Although you didn't believe me, did you?'

Bradley's smile faded for a second, but he quickly returned to it. 'Why, Charlotte, are you telling me off for such a slight mistake? Probably my interest was too taken up by you, rather than looking at the men wasting their time.'

She turned to Ned, who stood silently, listening to this little exchange. 'So, were you truly there, Mr Drake? Or was I just imagining someone dressed in your uniform?'

Ned's mouth twisted. 'Oh, come, Miss Westland, is it so important that you know all the details of my whereabouts? As a newcomer to the local Custom House I have many calls on my time. Certainly I have to visit certain people around the area, so perhaps you are correct, and you, Mr Reed, are wrong.'

And then Miss Felicia was hovering on the edge of the small group, holding out her hand

and smiling warmly at Ned, who bowed, was introduced, and at once began talking to her about the local beauty spots. 'Like me, Miss Felicia, I understand you and your brother are newcomers. Well, I can tell you that the bay is certainly very attractive—I have been along the cliff path which has a wonderful viewpoint or two.'

And Miss Felicia, her dark eyes alight with friendliness, said, 'As yet I have not ventured out, Mr Drake. There have been so many stories of smugglers along the coast that I feel we should all stay safely at home.'

'Ah, but, ma'am, my brave men will soon clear the seas of these wretched men and then you can take your ease everywhere in the village.'

Charlie watched Bradley's face as he listened. His mouth tightened, a quick frown darkened his brow, but then he was smiling again, as he said, 'This, of course, being the reason my sister and I invited you here this evening, Lieutenant, so that the village may know you are going to free us of these nuisances.'

Ah, thought Charlie, her mind suddenly alight with knowledge. So that is why Ned has been invited, for Bradley and Miss Felicia to let all their neighbours know that they are innocent of any crimes, and are relying on the Preventive Officers to scare off the so-called smugglers. And so—if Bradley himself is involved in smuggling, from now on no-one will suspect him. How clever! And how much I dislike him! Marry him? Never!

Madeira and sherry were being handed around and the conversation continued for another twenty minutes or so, with Charlie longing to somehow manage a private word with Ned, but not succeeding for Bradley seemed to have his eye on her all the time. Then dinner was announced.

'May I have the pleasure, Charlotte?' Bradley offered his arm, his smile very broad, and his dark eyes roaming all over her bare shoulders. Charlie could only accept, and so the small procession swept into the big dining-room, with Miss Felicia and Papa following Charlie and Bradley, Ned and Mrs Edwards next, and Jane and Dr Edwards, making a threesome with Harvey Jackson.

Charlie was led to the chair next to Bradley at the head of the long table, while Mrs Edwards sat on his other side, the other guests arranging themselves down the sides of the table.

Charlie, unused to formal dining of such a high degree, could only stare at the decorations in front of her. The long table was covered with a damask tablecloth and a battery of crystal glasses, silver cutlery outlining every dining placement, and a trail of green smilax wreathing in and out among the heavy candelabra and the dishes of fruit.

Bradley turned aside and said to her, in a low voice that she only just heard, 'Charlotte, there is something out in the garden that I should very much like to show you when dinner is over. Perhaps after you and the other ladies have taken coffee in the drawing-room, you might join me on the terrace?'

What could she say? Wishing that it were Ned making this suggestion rather than Bradley, she could only nod her head and murmur, 'Very well, just for a moment, perhaps,' wondering as she did so whether she was wise to agree to such a secret assignment and then it struck her, by some chance, had Bradley discovered that the lost jewel was in her possession?

For a moment Charlie trembled, but then the footman was at her side offering turtle soup and so she turned her thoughts to the moment. She was going to enjoy this delicious meal, come what may! Catching Jane's eye on the other side of the table, she made up her mind that somehow she would warn her friend of Bradley's intention to whisk her away into the darkness after dinner . . . she must be sure that, if needed, help would be at hand.

It was a relief when, at last, with plates empty, glasses drained, and most of the guests sitting back heavily in their chairs, that Charlie saw Miss Felicia look her way and raise an eyebrow. Then Aunt Jem glanced at her, also raising an eyebrow, and she understood that this was the sign for the ladies to leave the men to their walnuts and port and business talk.

Quietly, she stood up, nodding to Jane and Mrs Edwards to do the same, and then in a slow procession, the ladies left the room, Bradley holding open the door and looking at Charlie, as she passed, with a meaningful expression on his face. She knew what he meant, but made no sign of understanding. Instead, she waited just inside the drawing-room for Jane to join her, then drew her aside.

'I must speak to you. Quickly, before the others come.' They huddled behind one of the dark red velvet curtains that hung at the half-open french windows and Charlie whispered, 'Bradley has asked me to go out on the terrace. Please listen and watch and if anything strange happens, tell Ned what I have just told you.'

'Oh, Charlie, surely you shouldn't go outside with Bradley—and anyway, what does he want out there?' Jane's face was growing quite pink, and Charlie was quick to reassure her. 'Well, it isn't what you think, Jane, please remember that I really do dislike him—it's much more likely that he knows I have something of his that he wants returned . . .'

'What on earth are you talking about, Charlie?' But Jane's question remained unanswered as Aunt Jem, Miss Felicia and Mrs Edwards now came in, looking around them, and heading for the sofas and armchairs that filled the large, elegant room.

Miss Felicia lifted a small bell from the table beside her chair and rang it, ordering coffee when the maidservant appeared. Then, 'Come along, ladies,' she said, smiling, 'do sit down and let us discuss things that our dear brothers and husbands would have no interest in at all—Mrs Edwards, allow me to admire your beautiful dark blue dress with those lace panels and sweeping flounces. May I ask if you have a dressmaker in the village? If so, perhaps I might give her a few commissions.'

And then they were off. Silks, satins, laces, mantles, shawls and the latest fashion in bonnets. Charlie grinned at Jane and, when the maid came in with a silver coffee pot and beautiful small Worcester coffee cups, she took the chance to get up, seemingly to help hand around the cups, but actually to whisk through the half-open french window, behind the velvet curtains, and step out on to the terrace.

A white rose climbed the wall beside the window and she inhaled the warm, gentle fragrance with pleasure as she waited there. She supposed Bradley would appear soon, but what could he really want, out here?

When she heard a step behind her on the terrace, smelled the familiar pungent tobacco that he smoked, she knew he was there, so turned, 'Bradley? What do you want? I can't stay very long . . .'

The words were cut off as strong arms

clutched her, drew her away into the semi darkness of a large shrub at the far end of the terrace, and Bradley's gleaming eyes stared down into hers.

He said, very low, 'Charlie, I have to see you alone. I haven't been able to take my eyes off you all the evening. I have to kiss you . . .'

Charlie pulled away, but it was no good. He was too strong. She turned her head, feeling him draw closer still and thought desperately of how she could escape. Bradley's kisses were not what she longed for—oh, how foolish she had been to come out here! And she had thought it was all to do with the smuggled pearl . . . why on earth had she allowed herself to become part of his vile plot to get her alone? Struggling, she avoided his lips as he lowered his face towards hers, and was trying to decide whether a shout for help would land her in more trouble, when someone said, very close beside her, 'It's all right, Charlie. No-one's going to hurt you when I'm here.'

She recognised that voice, quiet, musical, but deeply felt, and at once knew she was safe. Ned wouldn't allow this bully to grab her any further. Indeed, she felt Bradley's hold on her loosen and then she was free, trying to escape and return to the house.

But, even as she approached the french window, she heard the scuffle in the bushes behind her, felt the strength with which Ned lashed out and hit Bradley's jaw. 'Don't touch her. I warn you, Reed, if you ever do this again, I'll do more than bruise you on the jaw.'

Then Bradley's footsteps were limping, disappearing off the terrace; there was a following quietness, through which she could hear the peaceful hum of voices in the drawing-room, and suddenly, she was in Ned's arms.

He held her for a long moment, whispering, 'Charlie, are you all right? That brute didn't hurt you?'

'No, Ned, he didn't, but thank goodness you came. Charlie relaxed in the warmth of his arms, reveling in his strength and in his obvious concern for her. But she knew that somehow she must find the strength to return to the house, so slowly she drew away from him, saying. 'I must go back. They'll all wonder what is happening.'

'And they mustn't know.' Ned's voice was for her ears only, but crisp and determined. He went on, 'Reed has disappeared for the moment, so we must pretend it was someone trying to break into the house who created a noise out here—you heard it and so did I, and that's why we are here now.' As she stepped away, he put out his hand, touched her shoulder. 'You're a brave girl, Charlie. Can you carry this off? Don't let anyone know what Reed was doing, for it would shock your family too much.'

She took a deep breath. 'I'll try, Ned. But

what is all this about?'

'I can't tell you—not yet. Just have faith in me, please. Go in and act your part, and as soon as I know where Reed has gone, I'll come back and tell the same story.'

They stood quite close, and she saw the expression on his shadowy face, warm and caring despite the seriousness of the situation. Her voice shook slightly as she whispered, 'Thank you, Ned, for rescuing me.'

He made no answer, but ran his fingers down her cheek and then nodded at her 'Go in, Charlie.'

As she entered the drawing-room she was met by a group of worried faces looking at the window. Her papa said quickly, 'I was just coming to find you, Charlotte. Did we hear noises out there? Are you all right?'

Somehow she found the strength to smile back at him reassuringly, smoothing her creased skirt as she did so, and say, 'Perfectly all right, thank you, Papa.' Behind her back she crossed her fingers and increased her smile. 'It was just that Bradley heard noises in the garden, and I went with him to see who it was. And then . .' she met Jane's eyes, saw doubt in them, and added, 'I told Jane I was going out to help, and I expect she told Mr Drake, who chased away the culprit.'

Miss Felicia's deep voice asked, 'A culprit? A thief? And who was it, pray? Has Mr Drake any idea why someone should come here and behave suspiciously on the terrace when we were all inside the room?' She paused and when no-one answered added rapidly, with a deeper note in her voice, 'Of course, they're after my jewels. It was the same in London, indeed, the reason we moved down here.'

Charlie saw people exchanging curious glances, and then Dr Edwards said quietly, 'No doubt there are rogues and vagabonds around in the countryside as well as in the town, Miss Felicia, and the lights from this room would be shining out for quite a distance.'

Then Charlie heard her papa add reassuringly, 'Quite right, of course. Far too many evil doers in the world around us. I see them in Court every week. And, I must say, well done, Mr Drake, for dealing with the matter.'

Charlie walked over to where Jane was standing and said brightly, 'I do hope that little incident hasn't stopped all our chances of dancing—don't you, Jane?'

Her friend picked up the suggestion eagerly. 'Yes, of course we must dance! We don't need any music, shall you and I start, Charlie? Why don't we sing, *Summer Is Icumen In*, like we used to do as children?'

At once Mr Jackson, standing close to her papa, began clapping his hands in the simple rhythm of the old folksong. 'How nice to hear some music, and we can all enjoy two pretty girls kicking up their heels, eh?'

The simple words sung in the girls' true, sweet voices, and the uninhibited movement of the old-fashioned dance gave a very satisfactory ending to what might have been a shocking scandal, had the true facts become known. As it was, Charlie managed to whisper to Jane in between verses, 'Everything is all right. Ned is out chasing Bradley somewhere . . . but we must keep the party going.'

So song followed song until even Charlie was thankful to sink down on to the big sofa and rest. Beside her Jane fanned herself and under cover of it, whispered, 'So where is Bradley? Charlie, I'm worried that he was hurt and needs attention . . .'

Charlie whispered back, 'Bradley is a wicked man and doesn't need any of your concern, Jane. He behaved badly out there on the terrace.'

The party was ending when suddenly the door flew wide and Bradley strode in. He had a large bruise around one eye and his mouth was puffed up. There were gasps of horror, and Miss Felicia caught her breath. 'Oh, my dear brother, what has happened? Are you badly hurt?'

'Not as bad as the other man, sister,' Bradley boasted, nodding at the surprised faces all around him. 'I took a slight punch— you can see the bruise—and he caught me on the side of my mouth, but otherwise I

134

suffered no ill. It was lucky that I heard the fellow before he tried to break in. No need for anyone to worry about me, but I thank you, friends, all the same.'

Miss Felicia was close to him, her hand on his arm, looking up into his battered face with a frown. 'And so you chased him off the premises? You and Mr Drake, together, I imagine.'

Bradley's smile changed into a tight lipped expression of irritation. 'Yes, Drake was there, too,' he said shortly, and the hard note in his gruff voice made Charlie ask the all-important question. 'And where is he now, Bradley?'

He turned to her, smiling again, as he said lightly, 'No doubt seeing to his prisoner. Back at the Custom House, I imagine. We shan't see him again tonight.'

'But we must express our gratitude to him, brother, for dispatching this rogue.' Miss Felicia's deep set eyes were gleaming in the candlelight and she stared at Bradley until he bowed his head, finally edging words out beneath his teeth. 'And what about gratitude to me? Drake was simply a last-minute help as I dealt with the situation.'

There were a few caught breaths from the remainder of the group as his words snapped out, and Charlie watched her papa and Harvey Jackson exchange understanding looks. She wondered whether Papa, with his instinctive ability to read characters, had at last realised just what a foolhardy and arrogant man Bradley was.

She hoped so, but then the door opened behind them and Ned came in, heading at once for his hostess, at whose side he stopped, saying, 'I'm glad to be able to tell you, Miss Felicia, that all is well. You'll hear no more of the culprit.' He turned towards Bradley, and said, sounding very serious, 'I fear you came off worse than either of us, Reed. But the bruises will go in time.'

But Charlie saw how his eyes lit up with satisfaction as he smiled before turning back to Miss Felicia.

'And I have missed the dancing, I believe? The maid who answered the door just now told me that the party was still continuing.'

Bradley and his sister looked at each other, and Charlie saw how Miss Felicia's mouth tightened as she nodded at him. 'We must have one last set of dances, I think, brother, so that Mr Drake can share the happy ending of our party. All we lack is the music . . .' She looked across questioningly at Charlie and Jane, and smiled, and that was all that was needed.

This time it was *The Sprig of Thyme* that Charlie began singing, and soon the room was once again treading the simple steps of the old folksong. And it was Ned who took Charlie's hand and swung her into the dance, while Bradley stood outside the circle, glowering and clearly impatient for the visitors to leave.

During the last few steps of the dance, Charlie managed to whisper to Ned, 'I have something extremely important to tell you. I'll be on the beach tomorrow afternoon . . .

So the evening ended, carriages rattling home and Miss Felicia and Bradley waving from the front porch as they left.

No-one spoke during their ride down the hill and into the stable yard, but Charlie's papa took her hand as he led her into the house, and said very quietly, 'A word with you, before bed, Charlotte. I think you may have something to tell me. Just say goodnight to your aunt and then come into the study.'

She was tired, but knew she must do as he asked.

'Sit down, Charlotte.' He smiled at her, sitting opposite in his big leather chair. 'Yes, I'm sure you are weary after all that dancing, but what enjoyment you and Jane gave to us all. And how well the party ended, after that unfortunate incident out on the terrace.' He leaned forward and looked deep into her eyes. 'Just what did happen out there, Charlie?'

Charlie, his old name for her. Suddenly she longed to tell him everything, but she knew that, should she do so, he would forbid any more meetings with Bradley—and if that happened it was unlikely that she would ever solve the problem of the smuggled pearl. For Thursday was only a few days away, and then she and Jane would be on board the schooner with Bradley, and surely while they were there for a few hours, she could find the next small piece of the puzzling jigsaw?

So, although her instinct was to tell all, she merely said quietly, 'Mr Drake was very brave and forced the burglar to run away, Papa. And then he followed him, and I suppose Bradley probably went indoors to bathe his wounds before joining us again in the drawing-room.'

She saw her papa's keen eyes narrow, but he nodded, and then, almost reluctantly, she thought, said, 'I see. So it was, in a small way, yet another adventure, my girl, was it? And one that you wish to keep to yourself, so as not to alarm either me or your aunt?'

Charlie heaved a sigh of relief. She knew that he probably guessed there was more to the incident than she was telling, but he had always allowed her privacy in her thoughts and some of her actions, so this was no different. Dear Papa. She got up, went close to him and put her arms around him, kissing his whiskery cheeks and saying, 'You're always so wise, Papa. And perhaps soon I shall be telling you a little more about my adventures . . .'

He seemed brighter then, she thought, and got up, his arm about her as they left the study and took the lighted candles waiting at the foot of the stairs. 'You know I trust you, Charlie, but I shall look forward to hearing whatever you decide to tell me.'

They parted on the landing, Charlie going to her room at the front of the house and he walking along the passage to his own room overlooking the garden.

Questions flashed through her weary mind. Was Ned really a Revenue Officer? Or could it be possible that he was, indeed, a smuggler? Taking off her gown and draping it over a chair, Charlie sighed deeply. Somehow it didn't matter which he was, for she was quite sure by now that she would always love him.

*   *   *

Aunt Jem looked at Charlie with an anxious expression as she came downstairs for breakfast in the morning.

'Dear child,' she said slowly, choosing her words with care. 'I am having grave doubts about your proposed trip out with Mr Reed in his boat tomorrow. In fact, in view of what happened last night, I feel it would be very ill advised of me, and your papa, to allow you to keep the engagement.'

Charlie felt a sinking in her stomach, but managed to keep a smile on her face. 'But why should you think this, Aunt? After all, last night is behind us, and there are no ill effects at all.'

Her aunt tightened her lips and was silent for a few moments while she poured the coffee. Then, 'Well, for one thing Mr

Reed was wounded and so may not be well enough to captain his boat. And, also . .' she stopped, spooned sugar into her cup, and then continued very slowly, 'I have a feeling that he is not quite the gentleman we all supposed him to be. Be should never have allowed you to follow him on to the terrace last night.'

Charlie thought quickly. 'No, Aunt. I suppose you're quite right. But I fear it was my foolish excitement over a possible adventure that made me insist on going with him. So please forget your unhappy thoughts. The Reeds, as Papa has told me, are gentlefolk with a good reputation and so you needn't worry about Jane and I going out with Bradley tomorrow.'

'Ah, well, it seems that you have made up your mind, and I know that nothing will change it now! You always had a strong will as a child, and I don't see any improvement these days . . .' But Aunt Jem was smiling and passing the toast rack over the table and Charlie heaved a sigh of relief.

'I do try not to be too wayward, Aunt,' she murmured, and was glad to see Aunt Jem's eyes twinkling as she changed the subject.

It was with a very light heart and a feeling of excitement that Charlie begged leave to walk on the beach with her shell bag after luncheon was over. 'Mrs Endacott has asked me to do some more shell arrangements, Aunt, and then, of course, I need more for the work in the grotto.'

'Very well. And when you come home at teatime we can discuss what you will wear tomorrow when you go aboard Mr Reed's boat.'

Charlie almost ran down to the beach, wishing, with a smile, that for this special occasion she could once again wear the old adventurous clothes, now hidden in her wardrobe. But then, her feet sinking into the soft sand, her eyes raking the horizon for a possible rowing boat heading for the bay, she forgot everything except that in a minute Ned would appear. And who would he be this afternoon? Smuggler or Revenue Officer?

When he arrived, it was, surprisingly, with another man. They came from the cliff path, making their way down on to the beach and then approaching Charlie as she bent and picked up shells to go into her bag. Both men were dressed in dull, shabby clothes and Charlie caught her breath—where was the handsome Revenue Officer uniform today?

Ned gave her a brief warm, almost intimate, smile, before introducing her to his companion. 'My friend, John Smiles. Both of us have knowledge of certain evil-minded people in the village. John, this is Miss Westland.'

Charlie bowed her head, wondering what sort of person this friend was, and watching as he nodded casually towards her. 'How do you do, Mr Smiles?' She paused; dare she ask the question that filled her mind? It wouldn't be denied. 'And are you, too, a smuggler?'

She thought he looked slightly embarrassed as he answered, 'Just an ordinary sort of working man, Miss Westland. Ned and I are trying to catch up with a band of newly come smugglers who are taking over this particular part of the Devon coast.'

Another secret, another disguise, thought Charlie, watching the quick glances between the two men. But why can't I be told the truth, whatever it is? She said rather snappily, 'So why are you here? They don't come by day, as you must well know?'

John Smiles grinned and Charlie thought quickly, a craggy face, quite handsome, but not as attractive as Ned. But he was continuing, 'But they off-load at night, Miss Westland, and Ned has heard from a local lad that they're using an old path leading to a secret tunnel. We're looking for it.'

Ben Luscombe, thought Charlie. She recalled the boy complaining about having to use that terrible path. And now he had told Ned about it .

'Through the Devil's Whisper, you mean?' she asked quickly. 'That horrid, steep little track leading to the path outside our houses on the cliff here?' Suddenly she was back there, hiding in the wild night, while the smugglers off-loaded their cargo.

John nodded. 'That's the one. Ned's been told that this path is in use after many years of neglect. I've come to try it out.'

Ned touched his shoulder. 'Go to the far side of the bay, John, around the corner, and there you will see the big cave. Go now, before the tide changes, otherwise I shall have to get out my boat and rescue you!'

Amid laughter, John Smiles touched his hat to Charlie, and headed for the rocks at the end of the bay. Ned; watching him go, then turned to her. 'Wonderful. Now I've got you to myself. Let's go and sit down where you can tell me the important thing you mentioned last night.' Together they walked to the far side of the bay, where they were almost hidden from view from anyone walking the cliff path, or coming down on to the beach.

Sitting close to Ned, their hands almost touching, Charlie said quickly, 'You weren't hurt last night, were you? I was so worried.'

He laughed. 'Not me, but Bradley Reed was, and I hope he'll remember that he must never take advantage of you again. He's a rogue, Charlie, and you would do well to keep away from him.'

Her heart sank. 'But I can't! Jane and I are going aboard his schooner tomorrow for a trip. We arranged it last week, and there's no reason to cancel it now, surely?'

Ned looked grave. 'Will his sister be there also? I don't like to think of you two young ladies alone with him.'

'We won't be alone, we shall have his crew around us, and yes, I think Miss Felicia said she intended being on board.' Charlie looked into his narrowed eyes. 'Why are you so worried, Ned?'

He didn't reply at once, but took her hand and stroked her fingers. Then, slowly, he said, 'Because I think I'm very close to finding this new gang who've taken over our local beaches, and certain facts tell me that he—perhaps both of the Reeds—are involved.'

Charlie gasped, and was silent, thinking hard. Then she said, 'What I have to tell you will, perhaps help in some way. You see, Andy and I have discovered a tunnel leading to the grotto in The Look Out grounds from the cliff path. The one you and your friend were talking about, I think. A horrid, narrow and dangerous little path leading into The Look Out grotto.'

Ned nodded. 'That's it. But what else, Charlie?'

She told him about finding the small package, and described what was inside its careful wrapping. 'A most beautiful pearl, a jewel, I suppose you would call it.'

'I would, indeed. And our newly arrived smuggling friends excel at landing rare jewels, for which they get paid exorbitant amounts from the rich people who want them so badly. But, Charlie . . .' He looked deep into her excited eyes. 'What have you done with this

144

pearl? Surely you don't carry it about with you? That would be most dangerous, for if the men who have lost it knew you had it, you would be in grave danger.'

A shiver ran through her and, as if he felt it, he put an arm around her shoulder. 'Be careful, Charlie,' he pleaded. 'You don't realise the wicked things these men will do if crossed.'

She smiled reassuringly. 'It's in a very safe place, Ned, in a small hidey-hole I discovered in one of the shell sculptures in the grotto. No-one but me knows it's there, but you could find it if you wanted. You could go to the grotto at night and search for it . . .' Her heart leapt. 'Why, perhaps I could come with you.'

'Charlie.' His smile was broad now and he shook his head. 'This isn't the time for pretending to be a cabin boy or whatever your disguise suggests. I would rather think of you safe in your home, not even looking out of your window at night.'

'Not even listening for your whistle, Ned?' she whispered.

'Not even that, sweetheart. We shall meet again soon, I'm sure of it. But until then promise me to take great care when you're On Reed's boat tomorrow. Stay with your friend, Jane, and don't allow yourself to be alone with him. A promise, please, Charlie . . .'

She leant against him, felt the warmth of his body, saw his shining eyes, and nodded as she realised the depths of his feelings and of her own. 'I promise, Ned.'

Gently he drew her close to him, cupped her face in his hands and slowly kissed her.

'So now I must go and find John and see what he has found out about the path. And you must go home, Charlie.' Together they walked back to where she had left her shell bag, and then he stopped, looking down at her.

'One other thing, Charlie.' His voice was firm, his smile had given way to a stern expression. 'I don't want you returning to the work in the grotto. Another promise, that you will stay away?'

'But the pearl that's hidden there . . . surely it must be returned to the rightful owner?' She felt very doubtful at having to give up her shell work, but he wanted a promise.

'Leave that to me. It will certainly go back to where ever it came from in the end, but the time isn't right.'

She longed to ask what that meant, and when the time would be right, but already he was looking over her shoulder and waving to John who had come out of the Devil's Whisper and was making his way across the beach to join them.

'Well, what do you think?' Ned said sharply, and his friend nodded. 'That's their route all right. We must be ready for the next trip.' The two men exchanged looks, and then Ned turned back to Charlie. 'Go home, sweetheart.

Enjoy your sailing trip tomorrow, and wait until I see you again.'

She left them talking in the middle of the beach and slowly, sadly made her way home, looking back over her shoulder as she walked up the cliff path, but no-one was there. They had disappeared and she was left alone with her head full of confusion.

From all Ned had said it seemed that he and his friend really were smugglers and trying hard to get even with the new gang who had taken over their landing grounds. It was possible Bradley and his sister also were smugglers, but surely, it wasn't possible—gentrified people like them, with money and position? Then perhaps she and Jane should not, after all, go aboard the schooner tomorrow, but to miss such an adventure!

Charlie went upstairs as soon as she returned to Headland House, putting her bag of shells away, sadly realising that because of her promise to Ned, she could take no more pleasure in restoring the old grotto.

Her head ached with all the thoughts whirling about, and she was quite relieved when Aunt Jem called her down to the drawing-room to discuss the clothes needed for the trip out to sea tomorrow.

'You have last year's best muslin dress which could well be covered with a shawl, or a cape. Winds can be very treacherous, you know, Charlotte. And you should wear shoes that will not slip on the wet decks. And, oh yes, a hat. No lady will go without covering her head, even on the water. Now, is there anything else you will need, I wonder?'

Charlie sat back in her chair and closed her eyes. 'I don't think so, Aunt. That all sounds very sensible.'

But she dreamed of one essential thing, and sadly knew it was out of reach. She wanted to be sailing, not with Bradley and Miss Felicia, but with Ned. And she couldn't help wondering if he still had thoughts of sailing away with her, one day? Sailing off to those foreign islands with their silvery sands and sunkissed lacy waves.

When Aunt Jem asked sharply, 'Is something wrong, Charlotte? You look quite dazed.'

She could only rearrange her face and murmur, 'No, Aunt, nothing at all.' But of course it wasn't the truth.

A DANGEROUS JOURNEY

Charlie awoke on Thursday morning with excitement racing through her. Breakfast was an annoying hindrance, and eaten hurriedly, much to Aunt Jem's disapproval, and then she ran upstairs again to put on her cloak, bonnet and winter shoes. Wide-eyed Susie, hovering on the landing as she went down into the hall again, said, 'Oh Miss, you look like someone going on an adventure,' and Charlie laughed happily.

'I am, Susie. Yes, I do believe I am!'

Outside, Eddie was waiting with the trap, and they drove down into the village to find Jane, who climbed in beside Charlie, and said nervously, 'Oh dear, I do hope I have enough clothes on, suppose we have a gale or something?'

Charlie's eyes sparkled as the trap bore them down into the harbour and the waiting long boat from Bradley Reed's schooner. She said firmly, 'Stop worrying, Jane, and just think about enjoying yourself. I know we're going to have a wonderful trip. Let's get into that boat, you go first and take the hand of that man who is waiting to help you.'

'Oh!' Jane wobbled and blinked madly as the boat moored at the harbour wall rose and fell with the lapping waves. 'Don't let me fall!' she cried, and the large man, dark haired, with huge hands, said soothingly as he helped her into the boat, 'Don't you fret, Miss, just get your sea legs and you'll be a happy maid. There, sit down, Miss, and I'll help the next young lady aboard.'

But Charlie was already jumping from the wall into the boat as the next big wave pushed it towards her.

'I see you're used to the sea, then.' The

big man watched admiringly as she found her way to the seat in the prow of the boat and sat down, tidying her skirts and cloak about her and then nodding reassuringly at Jane, sitting opposite and clutching the side of the boat with tight fingers.

'Yes,' said Charlie. 'I like boats, and being on the schooner is going to be quite an experience. Mr Reed is already aboard, I'm sure.'

He nodded. 'Aye, Skipper's up on the bridge. Tide's right and we'll be off.'

'And Miss Reed?' Charlie wondered if Miss Felicia really was accompanying them.

'Aye,' said the seaman again. 'The lady's in the cabin, awaiting you. Now, if you'm both settled safely, m'dears, I'll row you across to The *Seasprite*.' He sat down, pulled at the oars and then they were off.

The *Seasprite*, Charlie saw as they approached it, was a large and well-appointed schooner. Willing hands waited their arrival and first of all Jane, and then she herself, were helped up the rope ladder hanging over the side and there they were on the gleaming deck with Bradley at their side, all smiles, and dressed elegantly in navy pea jacket, canvas trousers and tricorne hat. 'Welcome aboard, ladies,' he said heartily, and conducted them on to the bridge where the man at the wheel saluted them, and then led them into the cabin.

Miss Felicia, very upright and dressed in dark bonnet and voluminous cloak, sat on the wooden seat lining the panels of the cabin, around the big central table. Her gleaming eyes warmed slightly as she saw them. 'Good morning to you, so you've got here safely. Bradley!' She raised her voice and her brother at once came to her side.

'We shall be quite happy here,' she said with a smile, 'so there's no need to worry about us frail creatures. I'm sure we are all far stronger than you imagine. Isn't that so, young ladies?'

Charlie exchanged glances with Jane, and said at once, 'Of course, Miss Felicia. I don't think either of us is likely to suffer from sea sickness.'

'We will sit here and watch through the portholes for sea birds as we sail out towards the horizon, brother. And you young ladies can entertain me by telling me what plans you have for your futures.' She turned to Bradley and said, half laughing, but her voice was firm and her eyes commanding, 'So back to the bridge with you, Captain Reed.'

Charlie saw how Bradley seemed to pause before smiling and nodding at his sister. She wondered which of the siblings held power.

'Now, about your futures; let us have a pleasant conversation. You, Jane, of course will become an artist. Is that not so?' Miss Felicia's deep voice brought a flush to Jane's pale cheek, but she nodded and said very quietly, 'I hope to do so, Miss Felicia. If I have the talent, that is.'

'And you, Charlotte. You will, of course, marry a man whom you know, and of whom your family approves, and lives near to your old home. Have you any thoughts about my brother, I wonder?'

Charlie stared into the dark, shimmering eyes looking into hers and wondered just what they were thinking. For a quick moment she felt a flash of horror at the idea of marrying Bradley and then Ned's face swam before her eyes. If only he were here . . .

Then, as her feelings calmed, she saw how Miss Felicia's arthritic fingers played with her huge rings and tried to understand exactly why she and Jane were being subjected to this intrusive questioning.

'I have no idea whom I shall marry,' she said lightly at last and saw the watchful eyes narrow slightly. 'But I hope to travel when I do marry. This village is very dull.'

'But not if you marry the right man,' cut in Miss Felicia quickly.

There was an awkward pause while both Jane and Charlie looked at their hostess.

And then Charlie felt herself become curious enough to ask the question. 'Why are you asking us such things, Miss Felicia?' she said bluntly.

The small woman sitting beside her squared her thin shoulders, looking even more erect than ever. 'Because they are important, my dear child. For what happens today may well affect both your lives.'

Jane gasped. 'What ever do you mean?'

'Well,' said Miss Felicia slowly, and with a smile spreading across her taut face. 'I must explain that the purpose of this invitation is to make you both understand that you are privy to some illegal happenings and therefore guilty of them.'

There was a sudden silence, tight and sharp, until Charlie said, 'You mean, of course, smuggling, don't you, Miss Felicia?' Recent facts churned around in her mind making a pattern, and then she gasped, saying, stunned, 'So you and your brother are trying to get us involved with your own lives, and the things you are doing in the village. And, why, now I know it, you are the smugglers who are trying to claim this bit of coast as your own!'

'So you know?' Miss Felicia clasped her hands together. 'I told Bradley you weren't the simple girl that your friend Jane is. Yes, we shall off-load our cargos whenever we wish, as we did the other night. And I believe, the next morning, that you found something in the grotto, didn't you?' Her voice grew harsh and she leaned towards Charlie. 'Come now, tell me exactly what you found and where it is now.'

Charlie rose from her seat and paced across the cabin, trying to sort out her thoughts. The boat had left harbour and was sailing slowly out into the wide expanse of ocean.

Every wave brought a lift and then a drop to the boat and her body moved with them. Suddenly she felt a great happiness engulf her. Yes, even although the Reeds were trying to trap her and Jane into becoming one of their wicked smuggling gang, she was enjoying herself. Such an adventure! And of course all their efforts would come to nought because she would refuse to play their game. She would never tell Miss Felicia about the pearl, hidden in the rose sculpture in the grotto.

Turning, she faced the little woman who watched so intently, and said firmly, 'You will never have the gem that was lost when the last lot of your contraband was off-loaded, Miss Felicia. That's what you are talking about, and I have no intention of telling you where it is.'

'Oh, but I think you will, you little fool . . .' The deep voice grew sharp, and the bony fingers reached out to clasp Charlie's arm. 'You see, we have the power to keep you here for as long as we think necessary. Until you decide to tell me about the gem . . . it was a pearl, wasn't it, a rare and beautiful one?'

Charlie felt a shiver of fear run down her back at the threat, but decided to keep Miss Felicia talking. 'Yes, an extremely lovely one, and I expect you were going to have it set into another ring, weren't you?' She saw the dark eyes widen, and added, 'as if your poor hands

154

needed any more weight on them . . . are you sure you have a finger which would take one more ring, Miss Felicia?'

Suddenly the hands clawed out at her more violently and she stepped back, out of their reach.

'How dare you!' cried the little woman, her voice rasping. 'You'll never know what it is to suffer like I do with my painful hands, and my rings are the only joys in life that I have left now I am growing old. You'll give me that pearl, Charlotte Westland, or else . . .'

Now Jane was beside Charlie and they clasped each other's hands as the boat began to roll more fiercely from side to side. 'Oh, Charlie, what is happening?' cried Jane. 'Why ever did we come? I want to go home . . .'

'Or else, what, Miss Felicia?' Charlie put her arms around Jane and persuaded her to sit down on the opposite side of the cabin.

'Or we'll make sure you never see your home again, you foolish girl. This boat is fully stored and ready for a long voyage. We can sail for as long as it takes you to decide to tell me about the pearl and where it is hidden?' Miss Felicia's expression was hard, her eyes gleaming with sinister intensity and Charlie felt herself slightly shiver. Could they really sail away, kidnapping her and Jane?

How she wished Ned was here; his strong arms protecting her, keeping her safe. If only he knew what was happening. But then her old courage returned, and she said quietly to Jane, 'Don't be afraid, she's talking nonsense. They can't possibly kidnap us. Someone will rescue us, of course, before very long . . .'

'But who will? Who knows we're here?' Jane was almost weeping.

Charlie thought hard. 'Our families know,' she said at last. 'And if we're not back when we said we would be, Papa will inform the constable, and the Revenue men and they will come looking for us . . .'

Miss Felicia's strident laugh made her bite off the unfinished sentence. 'What hopes you have, my dear! This boat will easily outrun any of the slow Revenue cutters! And it will be some time before your papa begins to worry about you, and we shall be long gone by then . . .' Her thin face softened into a smile of contempt and pleasure and Charlie felt rage growing inside her. Determination to escape created a plan of action.

She held Jane close and whispered, 'Go and sit down and talk to her; don't let her see what I'm going to do. Just keep talking. Go on . . .'

For a moment Jane stared blindly. Then she nodded slowly, and returned to her seat on the bench beside Miss Felicia, turning to her and saying, between several stammers and stutters, 'I think I may be feeling sea sick, Miss Felicia, can you suggest any remedy which might stop it?'

'What a helpless child you are! Lie down on

that bench over there—take a blanket to cover yourself; and stop thinking how ill you feel. Make up your mind to be strong.'

By this time Charlie had edged further to the closed door leading on to the bridge and suddenly took hold of the latch and threw it open. A blast of wind blew her bonnet askew and filled her skirts, but she kept her balance, stepping out on to the bridge.

She saw Bradley standing beside the man at the wheel, and quickly looked out to sea. The waves were getting higher, a mist had begun to drift from the quickly receding land, but she thought she saw, in the near distance, another boat. It was smaller than *Seasprite* and had not so many sails, but at least it meant she and Jane were not alone in this wilderness of waves and wind. It might even be a fishing boat with Andy sailing it . . . hope grew inside her.

Then her thoughts were dispersed by Bradley's voice roaring at hen 'Get back inside, Charlotte,' and he took hold of her shoulders, trying to bundle her through the still-open door, but somehow she resisted long enough to raise her arms and wave them as high as she could manage before he half carried her back into the cabin.

'You wretched girl!' he said curtly 'Stay there! I knew there would be trouble with you.'

Within his powerful grasp, Charlie found Bradley was no longer the handsome charmer she had at first thought him to be. Now his dark eyes raged at her, his strong hands bruised her arms, and he almost threw her across the cabin. 'Look after her, sister. I've got enough to do with keeping this boat on her course—don't let her out again.' He slammed the door behind him and Charlie was left, breathless but not defeated, sitting on the bench beside Jane who was hunched in her seat looking pale, but clearly trying to keep talking to Miss Felicia.

Charlie put her arms around Jane and hugged her close. 'Don't give up hope,' she whispered. 'I think I sent a signal to a boat which seems to be following us out there . . . it might be Andy.'

The movement of the boat grew stronger, the ship creaked and groaned as it rocked on the strengthening waves, and Charlie and Jane found it hard to remain seated inside the cabin. Miss Felicia, sitting as upright as possible on the opposite side of the little room, watched them with dark, narrowed eyes, playing with the huge rings on her small, bony fingers.

It seemed that several hours passed, but there was no clock in the cabin, and it was only when the movement of the boat calmed down a little, that Bradley appeared, closing the cabin door behind him, taking off his damp jacket and hat, and sitting at the table, looking at the girls opposite him. 'Well, ladies, enjoying your trip in the *Seasprite*, I hope.

Are you?' His voice was light and his smile the old charming expression that they both remembered so well.

But Charlie tightened her lips and refused to smile back. 'Your sister has told us that you are kidnapping us,' she said sharply. 'I demand that you take us back to shore at once. My father will have become anxious and will probably have started organising our rescue. If you don't return us immediately you will be in great trouble.'

To her annoyance Bradley put back his head and filled the cabin with loud laughter. Then he rose, came to her side and put an arm around her shoulders.

'I love your spirit, dear Charlie. When we are married I shall take you with me on our smuggling trips. You can dress up in your boy's clothes and act out the cabin boy role. You'll enjoy that, I'm sure.'

Charlie edged away from his embrace. 'I'll never marry you. Never!' she cried. 'And don't imagine that you'll be smuggling for much longer. Once the Custom Officers hear of this kidnapping you and your wicked sister will get your just deserts.'

'I don't think so, my dear.' Miss Felicia bent towards Charlie, nodding her head and smiling grimly. 'We are quite far from shore by now, and no Revenue boat can ever catch us. *Seasprite* has great speed, you see.'

Charlie, trying to avoid Bradley's embraces,

edged away from him, her mind in chaos. Supposing Miss Felicia was right—would she and Jane find themselves stranded on a foreign shore with no communication possible to their anxious families?

Then she heard the muffled roar of what sounded like gunfire. Her confusion grew. Was it a Revenue boat that she had seen in the distance, and not Andy? For a moment hope grew, but then she thought that, if the Reeds were right about *Seasprite*'s speed, then no-one could ever catch up with them.

And then, suddenly, there was another huge bang and the ship shifted with a rolling jerk that surprised them all. Jane nearly fell off the bench, Miss Felicia clung to her brother, and for a moment Charlie found herself flung against the table.

Bradley was up, pulling on his jacket, cramming his hat on to his head, striding out of the cabin and slamming the door behind him. In the cabin the three women stared at each other anxiously, even Miss Felicia's face turning pale. Jane clung to Charlie's arm. 'What on earth was that? Are we sinking?'

Charlie wondered the same thing, but managed to gather together her shreds of receding courage. 'Of course not, but it might have been gunfire. Don't worry, Jane. We'll be all right again in a minute.' But the minutes fled and more bangs and bumps threw them around the cabin, until, suddenly, the door flew open and two men came in.

Their faces were familiar. Charlie gasped with amazement and relief, for here were Ned and John Smiles and this time they were dressed in navy blue Revenue uniforms, and at their belts were pistols. She cried, 'Ned!' and couldn't stop herself rushing up to him, looking into his narrowed icy blue eyes and hiding her face against his shoulder to stop him seeing the tears that suddenly flowed. His arms were warm about her, and he whispered, 'Thank goodness you were brave enough to get on deck and signal. As soon as I saw you I ordered the gun to be aimed and then decided to board. Now you're safe, sweetheart.'

The next few minutes were chaos and she could only sink down on the wooden bench with Jane beside her, both of them staring as Bradley was dragged into the cabin by a couple more seamen with pistols in their belts, and watch him being interrogated by Ned, now sitting at the table and looking through the papers that lay there.

'So, Mr Reed, you are the owner of this boat? Are these its papers? Let me see them.'

In vain did Bradley start to argue and shout, even Miss Felicia joining in his raised declaration of innocence. 'How dare you board us like this! We are a private boat on private business. You have no right at all to be here! I shall complain to the Custom Officer when we return to shore.'

'Complain away.' Ned's voice was light and he raised an eyebrow in what Charlie imagined was amusement. He was sorting out the papers before him, and she wondered what he was looking for. Surely the ship's papers were evidence of what the Reeds had just insisted was the truth? But no, very slowly he stopped picking up different papers, and sat back in the chair, reading carefully one particular document, John Smiles at his side, reading over his shoulder.

Ned put down the paper, looked up at John and nodded. 'What we were hoping to find. We've got him, all right. And the lady with the jewels.'

Charlie's curiosity could wait no longer. 'What are you talking about, Ned? What have you found?'

Ned turned in his chair and smiled at her, and she saw from the excitement in his shining eyes that he had, indeed, found something really important. 'Charlie, this list of contraband is evidence of this man's, and his sister's, smuggling.' He lifted the document and waved it triumphantly. 'And here is something even better—a list of the owners of the various items run ashore the other night together with the men who did the smuggling. Everything we need to prepare a strong case against these two wretches is here. No magistrate can possibly deny the authenticity of the names and addresses on this list.

Look, John—' He raised a finger, pointing to different items on the paper. 'Lafarge from Brittany with his three hundred tons of tobacco; Mr Gunter who had gems stolen in Holland and then smuggled ashore here, and a huge consignment of lace from the Channel Islands, which, it says here, is transported inside fifty carcases of turkeys . . .' He laughed. 'Imagine the stench of that particular bit of contraband!'

Charlie joined in the laughter as the tight band of despair and fright which had been building inside her for the last hour or two finally disappeared, in its place dawned a wonderful new sense of hope and happiness. Ned, dear Ned, whether he was smuggler or Revenue officer, she still was unsure, but did it matter? He had rescued her and Jane, and had put in place more pieces of the puzzling jigsaw. How right she had been in thinking that a trip in *Seasprite* might help resolve a few problems.

But Ned still had more to tell them. He picked up a last piece of paper and turned towards Miss Felicia, still erect in her seat on the wooden bench. 'And here is the evidence of a smuggling venture which involves you, Miss Reed, even more than your brother. I have proof of your activities in London, where you were the mistress of an international jewel smuggling gang. Written evidence, too, of the capture of a couple of your men who gave information about you to regain their freedom, and as a result of which, you and your brother had to flee from the city. Which I now understand is the reason you came down to Devon, planning to continue your activities at The Look Out.'

Miss Felicia was silent for a second or two, her face contorting into rage, her hands clenched in her lap. Then, abruptly, she spoke quietly, but with dull hatred in her voice, 'You think you are very clever. I don't deny my leadership of the jewel gang, just look at what I have on my fingers, proof of my ability to find and take for myself fine jewels worth a fortune.' She opened up her hands, flaunting her heavily laden fingers in his face, her expression sneering and full of pride.

Furious at this attack on Ned, Charlie was quick to retaliate. 'But the one jewel you longed for, Miss Felicia, the rare pearl which I found in the grotto, and which is safely hidden where no-one but me can find it, will never be yours.'

She flinched at the look the little woman gave her, and Ned cut in quietly. 'Indeed, that is so, because here we have the name and address of the man who owned it before it was smuggled out of Holland, and I shall make sure that it is returned to him.' He turned to Charlie, and smiled at her. 'So I shall have to ask you, Miss Westland, to take me into your confidence and tell me of the hiding place.'

They exchanged looks for a moment,

concealed smiles that Charlie wanted to go on and on, but then Ned said, 'And now we must arrange the return of this boat and her kidnapped visitors safely to shore, while I take the Revenue cutter and sail back to the Custom House.' Rising, he took Charlie's hands and drew her towards the cabin door. 'Come with me, Miss Weston, I have something private to say to you.'

Out on the bridge, he turned his back on the man at the wheel after giving him instructions. Then, taking her along the deck, where she saw the damage of the gunfire, and into the shelter of the main-mast, he put his arms tightly around her and said, above the noise of the wind and the flapping sails, 'Charlie, I have to leave you, but John Smiles is a good man and will safely return you and Jane to your homes.' He paused, cupped her face in his hands, and said tenderly, 'Are you quite sure that Bradley Reed didn't harm you in any way?'

Charlie rested against his strong body and looked into the caring blue-green eyes. 'No,' she whispered. 'He tried to kiss me, but I got away . . . Oh, Ned, must you go now? Can't you take us home? I'm sure your friend, John, is a good man, but I want to be with you.'

Ned sighed and held her tightly for a final kiss. 'I shall be with you again soon, Charlie. Believe me. 'Ned's hands were firm about her, but he took a step away. 'I can't tell you any

165

more. You must trust me, but I promise I shall see you soon.'

She was led back along the windswept deck and left in the warm, dry cabin, where she found Jane sitting alone and looking upset. 'Oh, Charlie, where did you disappear to? I have missed you so much.'

Charlie looked around her. All the papers had disappeared, and she realised they had been removed for taking to the Custom House as evidence against the Reeds. She wondered where Bradley and his sister had gone and asked Jane, who said unevenly, 'John, I mean Mr Smiles, took them away to be imprisoned below, while we sail back to shore, following Ned in his boat.'

Charlie shut her eyes, picturing Ned's dangerous descent of the rope ladder to the small boat lurching between the cutter and the schooner. She shivered, but the door opened and John Smiles came in. He said, 'The prisoners are safely below, and the galley is cooking a hot meal which will be brought to you very soon. Meanwhile, please try and make yourselves as comfortable as you can. Miss Westland, is there anything I can do for you?' When Charlie shook her head he turned to Jane, his smile warm. 'And what about you, Miss Edwards? Perhaps an extra coat to keep out the cold?' He opened a door at the end of the cabin, found an old jacket, and very carefully put it around her shoulders.

Charlie watched as Jane's pallor turned into a warm blush, and thought, with relief, that perhaps her friend's passion for Bradley had died. She hoped so. Certain John Smiles seemed a far nicer and more suitable admirer, but this turned her thoughts again to Ned, now sailing away into the distance, and she sighed. He had said she would see him soon, but when would that be?

SAYING GOODBYE

HOME. Charlie could hardly believe her happiness and good fortune at being back at Headland House with Aunt Jem and Papa, and Susie, in the kitchen, fussing over her.

'Are you sure you feel quite well, Charlotte? You look a little pale, and you're wet through ...' Once Papa, waiting in the harbour with the trap, had driven the rescued girls home, Aunt Jem's eagle eyes swept over Charlie, from her salty, tangled hair to her heavy cloak and damp winter shoes. 'Susie will take up hot water and you must have a bath and then, I think, bed. What a terrible shock you have had, dear child.' Aunt Jem was near to tears, and Charlie somehow stopped herself from refusing to be sent to bed so early in the evening. But yes, she had to admit it had been a shock, all that rolling about on the wild ocean, and then the horror of knowing exactly what Bradley and his wicked sister were planning.

And then she lay back in the bath in her bedroom, and closed her eyes. To counteract all that dreadful experience, there was the joy of seeing Ned again Of his kisses. Of his promise—*'Soon, Charlie, very soon . . .'*

Another flash of memory, of Papa's bear-like hug and his unsteady voice. 'Charlie! My dear daughter. Thank goodness you're safe—I will always be grateful to who ever stopped those terrible Reeds from making off with you. Once you're home and warm and dry I shall send a message of congratulations and thanks to the Custom House, telling who ever was responsible for saving you that I owe him a great debt and would like to meet him in person.'

Then Susie's voice banished the memories. 'Will you get out the bath now, Miss? I've got the towel and it's nice and warm . . .' Enveloped in a thick pink towel, Charlie felt her body responding to its familiar, safe environment. She was back in her own bedroom and Ned had said he would see her soon. Aunt Jem had grudgingly agreed to her going downstairs for dinner, and tomorrow she would go to the grotto and make sure that the pearl was still safe. Ready to give it to Ned, when she saw him. *When . . .*

At dinner—a good hot meal of braised lamb washed down with a celebratory glass of red wine—Aunt Jem and Papa asked Charlie for every detail of her kidnapping. Which made her thoughts turn to Jane. Poor Jane who had been even more scared than she had, but who had done her best to not to show her fear. Charlie smiled happily, recalling how Jane had plainly depended on John Smiles to help her disembark, before her father drove her home, and had given him a last look which surely meant she had fallen for him. Better John Smiles than Bradley Reed, thought Charlie draining her glass, and then, like a black cloud, yet again came the thought that John, like Ned, was a smuggler. Or were they both Revenue officers? Would she ever know the truth about them?

But a good night's sleep worked wonders and the next morning she was up in good time for breakfast, despite Aunt Jem's orders last night to stay in bed until midday, saying firmly, 'You must get your strength back, my dear.'

Well, it had come back now, thought Charlie, dressing and planning to make her escape to the grotto as soon as Papa and Aunt Jem were engaged in their daily duties. After what she had heard about the stolen gem stones, she could hardly wait to have another look at the pearl and to make sure its hiding place was truly safe.

The Look Out was quiet and as she walked through the garden, Charlie felt a strange emptiness about the whole place. Of course, the Reeds had been captured and taken, she supposed, to Exeter, to be charged with their crimes of smuggling and attempted kidnapping.

Charlie paused in the entrance to the grotto, looking behind her at the greenery of the garden as it sloped down towards the cliffs, and wished that, somehow, she could bring peace to the little ghost that all the villagers said haunted the old house. Surely there was something she could do to bring an end to the sad tale? Thinking hard, she went into the grotto and stood in front of the rose panel, admiring the expert work which had sculpted such a perfect flower, and wishing that the tragic love story could have, even now, a happy ending.

And then, suddenly, and clear enough to turn her sharply around, a step sounded on the path outside. She caught her breath. Mr Reddaway, wondering if she needed more mortar, perhaps? Even curious Andy, wanting to hear all about yesterday's shocking adventure? Charlie smiled briefly, knowing, of course, that the story must be all about in the village.

But it was Ned who stood there, smiling at her, his eyes as brilliant as the blue sun-kissed sea, holding out his arms and enfolding her in a strong embrace as, without thinking any more, she moved into them. For a moment neither of them spoke. Charlie lay her head

170

against his chest and heard the steady beating of his heart, felt the warmth of his body and knew herself safe and loved. What more in the world could she want? She raised her head and offered him her lips. Their kiss was deep and wonderful.

And then Ned said, very quietly, his mouth close to her ear, 'Dearest Charlie, thank goodness you're safe. I had some terrible moments when we were chasing that schooner, but the old Revenue cutter wasn't flying the golden Customs flag for nothing, and I knew we should eventually win.'

Charlie rested in his arms, her mind at ease, her body full of glorious sensations of joy. But then she saw his smile fade, watched his brilliant eyes narrow and grow shadowed and felt fear clouding her happiness. 'What is it?' she whispered. 'Something's wrong. What is it, Ned?'

He didn't reply at once, but when he did his voice was low and quiet. 'I have to go away, sweetheart, I can't tell you for how long. But I must go.'

She released herself from his arms and stepped back, staring in disbelief 'But where? And why? Ned, please tell me the truth about who you are.'

She saw his face tighten, felt his hands reaching out for hers, and knew herself once again in that unhappy abyss where mystery and worry reigned supreme. And she had just thought she was safely loved and happy. Then it came to her that she was feeling the wretchedness of the little girl, Rosina, who had loved and lost. Was this happening to her, too? Yes, she loved Ned, but she was about to lose him.

He said slowly, searching for every word, and holding her hands tightly in his own, 'I can't answer that, Charlie. I have to go away, but I can't tell you where to, or why. But, sweetheart—' He pulled her closer, whispering gently as he did so, 'I think you love me and trust me, so I can only ask you to wait.'

'To wait? You mean there's a chance that you'll return?' Hope was flooding in and she heard her voice rise.

He nodded. 'Yes, just a chance. Charlie, you must go on waiting.'

She blinked away the tears that made her eyes swim. 'I will. Of course I will. For ever, if need be.'

They kissed again, and then he drew her into the grotto until they stood before the rose sculpture panel. 'You told me about the pearl, Charlie, and its hiding place. May I ask to see it?'

Her thoughts leaving the enveloping sadness of the last few moments, she removed the centre of the flower and drew out the pearl. It gleamed in the sunlight that shone through the open doorway, and she and Ned looked at it very intently. Then, with it in his hand, he asked, 'Will you let me take it, Charlie? As a smuggled jewel it must be taken to the Custom House for proof of its identity.'

She was sad to think that the beautiful, glistening pearl must leave what she thought of as its natural home in the centre of the rose, but she understood the need to have it shown to the authorities. She smiled a little apologetically, for it seemed all her dreams were fading, both for herself and for poor Rosina. 'I had thought it might help the little ghost to find happiness after all, you see.'

Gravely, Ned nodded, still examining the exquisite pearl resting in his hand. 'A lovely thought, sweetheart, but I don't think it can happen.' He smiled down at her.

'I shall wait, Ned,' she said, very low, and they kissed again.

And then he was gone. Just his footsteps fading down the garden path, and the centre of the beautiful rose empty and needing to be filled again with mortar. No more a hiding place, just a sad centre of a flower that was now only half finished. Charlie dried her eyes, told herself she must be brave, as brave as she was on *Seasprite* when Bradley was threatening her, and then left the grotto to its memories.

Back at Headland House she forced herself to remain cheerful, knowing that she had so much to be thankful for, and Ned had asked her to wait.

She was glad when, after luncheon, Aunt

173

Jem took her into the morning-room and said firmly, 'You must try to forget the awful past, Charlotte, my dear. And to that end I have a very nice occasion waiting for you. The midsummer ball in a week's time.' Her eyes were bright, her smile encouraging.

Charlie thought back and then remembered Mrs Albert pinning the hem of the pale blue muslin gown. It seemed so long ago now. She had not then been particularly excited about the coming ball, but now it was a sort of godsend, taking her thoughts away from Bradley and Miss Felicia, even allowing Ned to fade into the background for a while. She smiled at Aunt Jem and ordered her thoughts. Yes, the new gown with its floating tulle trimmings. The family pearls. The need to make herself look as pretty as possible. And she decided she would try her hardest to please Papa and Aunt Jem and show them just how grateful she was for their love and care.

She said, 'I wonder if my new ball gown is finished now? Shall I go and call on Mrs Albert? Oh, and I must see Jane, too, for, of course, she will be coming to the ball.' At once her thoughts became more cheerful. She had much to talk about with Jane, and it would be a good idea to walk down to the village and call on her this afternoon.

Aunt Jem approved the idea, saying, 'Mrs Albert will be here first thing tomorrow morning to fit the dress and make any

174

alterations that are necessary. So you have plenty of time to sort out exactly what you plan to wear with it. Your white satin slippers? Something to decorate your hair? And of course, your gloves and opera cloak . . .' She looked at Charlie lovingly. 'But first of all go and find your friend, for I'm sure you need to talk to each other. I do hope Jane has recovered from the awful experience, for she's not nearly as adventurous as you are, my dear child.'

Charlie got up and went to the door, saying over her shoulder, 'Jane was very brave on board the *Seasprite*, Aunt. And I think the experience might well have changed her mind about a few things.' Like finding Bradley attractive, for one thing.

Walking down the path to the village, Charlie suddenly found herself to be full of new hope and even a touch of excitement about the coming ball. After all, life had a strange habit of throwing unexpected things at one, didn't it? So what might happen next, she wondered?

AN UNEXPECTED APPEARANCE

Jane was sitting at her easel in the little studio at the back of the garden. She put down her brush when Charlie arrived and said unsteadily, 'I was thinking of coming round to see you and here you are. Oh, Charlie, I don't think I shall ever get over that terrible time on the boat, with those rolling waves, and, and . . .' Her voice broke.

Charlie put her arms around her friend and said soothingly, 'But of course you will, Jane. It's all over now and we're both home and safe, And those dreadful Reeds will never bother us again.' Then she added, 'And now show me what you're painting. Why, it's the wild sea and the *Seasprite*. Jane, it's very good indeed. Surely the best picture you've ever painted. And look, that man, there, on the deck, don't I recognise him?'

She saw Jane blush, but look happier, as she said firmly, 'I hope you do, Charlie. It's Mr Smiles. You see, I needed to have a figure on the boat and . . .'

'And,' finished Charlie, grinning, 'he's the one who has stayed in your mind, hasn't he?'

'Well, yes,' admitted Jane, but she was smiling now and her voice was more cheerful. Charlie sat down on the floor beside the easel, and looked up into her friend's face. 'Jane, what are you wearing to the county ball on midsummer eve?'

'Goodness, don't know. I had quite forgotten about it. But, yes, I must think very seriously. Perhaps my pale green taffeta or possibly the pink tarlatine and lace with the gauze flounces. What about you, Charlie?'

'A new pale blue finest muslin decorated with tulle trimmings that is being made for me.' Charlie's smile faded, and she looked at Jane with an expression of resolution. 'We have to forget what we've been through. Although Ned has gone away, and I wonder if I shall ever see him again.'

Jane cleaned her brush in the pot of water and then looked back at Charlie. Her voice was quiet, but her eyes were calm. 'And I shall possibly never see John Smiles again. You're right, Charlie, we have to forget.'

The two friends nodded at each other and then were silent for a few moments, until Jane said determinedly, 'So thank goodness we have the ball to look forward to. Let's talk about it instead of worrying, shall we?'

And that is just what they did for the rest of the afternoon. Gowns, cashmere shawls, paisley wraps, hair decoration, fans, gloves, jewels . . . it was teatime before they knew it and Charlie went back to Headland House with her mind full of happier things than missing Ned. But, of course, once she was in bed that evening, the memories returned. His brilliant eyes. His warm kisses. Then, somewhere, echoing behind those lovely images, his last words. *I can only ask you to wait.* And yes, like a cloud at the back of her mind, the terrible thought that she might wait for ever.

Mid summer day dawned full of hazy mist,

through which the sun soon shone its brilliant rays, bringing warmth and a special beauty to a day just asking to be celebrated. Charlie worked at a new shell flower arrangement in the morning, and then, as Aunt Jem ordered, rested quietly until teatime, her mind busy planning more craft work. She knew she must keep busy to avoid slipping hack into unhappiness over Ned's disappearance.

Then it was time to dress. Susie was at hand to do up the small pearl buttons that fastened the beautiful new pale blue muslin gown all down its back. 'My, Miss Charlotte, but you'll have to take a breath in if I'm going to fasten this last button . . .' But small, deft fingers finally completed the task, and then Charlie's hair was dressed as she sat in front of the dressing table and its three-sided mirror.

Her hair decorated, and thinking Susie's arrangement was very elegant, Charlie stood in front of the big pier mirror by the window, looking at herself. Yes, Mrs Albert had made a wonderful gown. The muslin floated around her like a drifting cloud, and the tulle scallops around the full hem, which matched the fluted fichu around the low neckline, allowed the gown to blossom out beautifully.

Aunt Jem would soon appear, bringing with her the family string of pearls which would go around her neck and so complete the picture.

'Gloves, Miss Charlotte?' Susie was holding out long white gloves which Charlie very carefully rolled over her hands and up her arms. She looked down at her feet and saw the toes of her pristine white satin slippers just slipping out from beneath the scalloped flounces of the gown.

'Oh, Miss, you look just lovely . . .' Susie breathed and Charlie told herself that, yes, she did look nice. And wouldn't it be wonderful if Ned could see her looking like this? But then she bravely pushed away the thought. Tonight she must just enjoy meeting her friends, chatting, dancing and then sampling the refreshments and the champagne. It was important to forget all the sad memories.

Then Aunt Jem knocked and entered the room, holding out the pearl necklace. 'Allow me to fasten this for you, child.' Her voice was warm and her eyes loving. Charlie felt emotion sweep through her as the necklace was clasped behind her neck, and realised that it had decorated many a young girl in the family, including her mother, before her. This was a cheerful thought, and she followed Aunt Jem down the stairs and into the waiting carriage with a heart full of expectant happiness.

The Assembly Rooms in the nearby town were alive with glowing lights and chattering voices. When the carriage halted at the entrance Papa descended and helped Aunt Jem and Charlie down. They went into the foyer and then into the ladies' cloakroom where they left their wraps, and then found him waiting for them ready to take them into the big chamber where the members of the local council sat in a welcoming group. Of course, everyone had learned about the *Seasprite* and the wicked action of Bradley Reed and his sister, so Charlie soon had a gathering of friends around her, longing to hear all the details of the proposed kidnap. She was thankful after a little while to excuse herself and go across the floor to where Jane and her parents sat on small gilt chairs.

She thought Jane looked prettier than usual, with fresh colour in her cheeks and a dress that swayed prettily with every graceful movement. They sat, fans in their hands and chatted for a few minutes, then the music started. A small orchestra was grouped behind rows of pots of flowers and ferns, and soon the dancing began. Charlie watched young men approaching her friends and asking for their dance cards.

She saw attractive smiles and blushing faces, and wondered who would come and ask her for a dance. Jane caught her eye and they looked at each other, knowing that their thoughts had met; where were Ned and John?

Surprisingly Charlie saw Papa approaching from the foyer, working his way around the dance floor, followed by two tall men in splendid uniforms. At first she wondered who they were, but then Jane was on her feet, smiling and saying excitedly, 'John!' and at once Charlie recognised John's companion as

Ned.

She jumped up, hardly able to restrain herself from running straight into his arms, but Jane was clutching her arm. 'Wait, wait!' she whispered. 'They're coming over here!'

And indeed, they were, heading for the row of gilt chairs. As they neared, Charlie saw the warm expression on Ned's face and felt her own smile answering it. Her heart leapt. He was here! But in yet another disguise . . .

Both men wore the Mess dress of the Royal Navy. Their strong figures looked even more handsome than usual in loosely unbuttoned blue coats with scarlet facings. White breeches and stockings stretched down to highly polished black shoes and gold epaulettes shone on their shoulders. Tricorne hats were held beneath their arms, and small stripes of lace decorated the coat sleeves.

Charlie felt she was in a dream—a wonderful, blessedly happy dream—meeting Ned's bright eyes and understanding what he was feeling at this strange and marvellous moment. But Papa was speaking and she had to force herself to concentrate.

'Charlie, my dear. I have just had a huge and most welcome surprise. I have met these young men who helped rescue you and Jane from the *Seasprite* the other day.'

'But where did you meet them, Papa? Did you go to the Custom House to find them?' Charlie's heart began to sing as she smiled brilliantly at him.

'I did indeed, but at the Custom House they refused to give me any information. It was all most strange, and I began to wonder about the backgrounds of those young men. Indeed, it came into my mind that they also were smugglers, simply trying to fight off a rival gang, yet had the goodness to rescue you and your friend.

'Perhaps they were thinking they would be rewarded for such a noble action and after much thought, I decided that seemed to be the answer to the question.' Papa's eyes were twinkling, and after a pause, he went on, 'but then, this very evening, I was called into the foyer and told two gentlemen wished to speak to me. And, my dear, here they are. Allow me to introduce them—Lieutenant John Smiles and Captain Edmund Drake, officers in the Royal Navy, both courageous and clever young men who have been working undercover to try and search out and capture the Reed family gang of smugglers, which they have now successfully done.'

Charlie heard Jane give a gasp and turned to her friend. At last the puzzle was resolved and their families could meet both John and Ned. 'Jane, take Lieutenant Smiles and introduce him to your mother and father, sitting over there. And Papa, please tell Aunt Jem who Ned really is and then perhaps we can thank them both properly for their bravery and cleverness.'

Papa nodded, and escorted Jane and John to where Dr and Mrs Edwards were sitting, watching their daughter with wondering eyes. Charlie knew there must be all these conventional introductions and explanations, but she was full of longing to take Ned somewhere where they could be alone together. Ned, or should she call him Edmund now? No, he would always be Ned.

The two families talked at length, even as the dancing continued all around them and the heat of the room grew, bringing fragrance from the many ladies' corsages. It was a heady atmosphere, and slowly Charlie's thoughts expanded to a need to be held in Ned's arms, to dance with him among the throng of couples filling the ballroom.

Did he read her thoughts? Were her eyes sending him a message? She would never know, but he was at her side, bowing, asking, 'Miss Westland, will you do me the honour of dancing with me?'

Her reply was swift, her smile radiant. 'With pleasure, Captain Drake.'

He opened his arms, led her on to the floor and swept her off in a dance that had her feet hardly touching the ground, her face upturned to his and their expressions reflecting one another's happiness.

As the music ended Ned very briefly held her close to him and whispered, 'We have so much to talk about, sweetheart—but this isn't the place. How I wish I were trotting my horse along the cliff path and whistling beneath your window. Would you run down and come to me, Charlie?'

'Of course I would! Nothing would stop me. But surely we can meet again soon?'

He nodded, taking her back to the waiting gilt chair. 'I have some duties to perform first, some problems to resolve about the smuggled contraband that the Reeds dealt in, but I shall be back.'

Charlie's happiness faded a little. She wanted him to be here, all the time, but of course as a Naval Officer he had many responsibilities which must come before her longing. When would he be back? And for how long must she wait? She supposed that, as the Captain of a naval ship, he would probably be sailing off somewhere shortly. She sighed deeply. Would she be left, waiting again? Could she bear it? And supposing Ned's ship didn't come back for months? What would she do without him?

But she had learned many lessons over the last months, and now she knew that she must let him go without any complaints. So she smiled into his keen sea-blue eyes and said very quietly, in a composed voice, 'I shall count the moments until you come back, dear Ned. Just don't let it be too long.'

She watched him turn away and speak to

her papa and wondered what he might be saying. Then he and John made their farewells to the two family groups, explaining that they had to return to duty. She saw Jane looking up into John's smiling eyes and knew that her friend was feeling the same desperate loss that she herself felt. Would John come back to Jane?

Which brought the same old question—when would Ned come back to her? And then he was standing in front of her, bending over her offered hand, and whispering, 'I shall see you tomorrow, Charlie. You see, I shall be calling on your papa. I have a very important question to ask him.'

A VOYAGE OF DISCOVERY

A new day and Charlie was up with the dawn chorus, leaning out of her window, breathing in the warm, fresh air and wondering when Ned would come to ask Papa what he had said last night was an important question.

Could she guess what it was? Dare she? She was all smiles but full of nervous hopes and fears when, after breakfast, she heard horse hooves in the yard, then voices in Papa's study and went out into the hall, hiding herself in the shadow of the grandfather clock in the far corner.

Would Papa and Ned never stop talking? Why didn't they come out of his study? The minutes seemed like hours, but at last the door opened and there was Papa, looking around as if he knew she was hiding somewhere. And Ned was behind him. Smiling . . .

Charlie flew into Papa's arms. 'Did he ask you? And did you say yes? Oh, Papa, tell me, for goodness' sake!'

'Dear child, I did say yes. But now the young man must ask for himself—why not go into the garden and talk?'

In the cool shadow of the yew hedge that sheltered the vegetable patch from the summer borders, on a wooden bench seemingly made for secluded conversations, Ned went down on one knee, holding her hands in his and asking unsteadily, 'Charlie, I love you so much and I want you to marry me.' He paused, looking into her brilliant eyes and then added, 'It will probably be another adventure, but what do you say, Charlie, my sweetheart?'

Only one thing to say and it left her lips with heartfelt happiness. 'Yes!'

He got up, drew her from the bench and kissed her, his lips warm and tender, growing stronger as he felt her joyful response. When Mr Reddaway appeared around the hedge, saw them, touched his hat, murmured an apology, and retreated, neither of them saw him, so engrossed were they in this wonderful moment.

But then, as their senses returned to everyday problems, they talked. Yes, they would marry as soon as possible, in the village church, with a small reception here at home. Then Ned had to leave the country on another mission overseas. Perhaps Charlie would like to find a little house, not far away, in which she could settle, awaiting his return on leave?

At first she said yes with delight, but then, after Ned had left, saying he had some important business to complete before he would be free again for the wedding, she sat there in the sun, thinking over what they had arranged. And wondering . . .

They married on a warm July morning in the little nearby church, with all the villagers who knew them gathered around the churchyard, waiting to see the bride and her handsome groom. Susie and Cook sat at the back of the church, with Eddie, the groom, near the door waiting to drive the newlyweds home after the service. Charlie wore a white dress cut from her mother's wedding dress, with orange blossom in her hair, and was attended by Jane, wearing her ball gown, and who smiled shyly at John Smiles, the best man. Charlie walked up the aisle on Papa's arm, and passed Aunt Jem in the first pew, wiping away tears but smiling at the same time.

The service ended, she and Ned, now man and wife, so the vicar told them with his blessing, went out into the sunlit churchyard and smiled at the waiting villagers. The Reddaways, the Endacotts, school children and their teachers, fishermen leaving their net mending on the beach—they were all there and their voices joined in wishing good luck to the happy pair.

The reception was pleasant, with Cook's special dishes on the buffet and Papa's expensive champagne—'Not smuggled, my dear,' he whispered, smiling at Charlie. The cake was cut with Ned's sword and Charlie thought she would burst with happiness.

Once all the guests had disappeared and they were left alone in the garden. When Ned said he had something to tell her, Charlie sat down quietly beside him and listened.

'Your pearl,' he began, looking at her very seriously, 'must go home to its owner.'

'Its owner? But how ever did you find him?' Charlie was aghast, feeling just a little sad that poor Rosina would now never have the jewel left in her rose sculpture.

Ned looked very serious. 'The papers Reed had on his table in the cabin of the *Seasprite* which I took with me when I left, told me a lot about the people who actually owned the contraband he and his gang off-loaded. Even gave me an address or two. So I was able, after a lot of work, to send a letter to the Mr Gunter who was robbed of this pearl, telling him I knew of its whereabouts now.'

'And he replied?' Charlie was intrigued.

'He did. Just a few days ago and, Charlie, although I know you won't want to part with your lovely pearl, I'm afraid you must. He is delighted to think it will be returned to him.' Ned was looking at her rather anxiously, she thought, and felt a jolt of sadness at the idea of having to part with it.

He took her hands in his and held them to his chest. 'My darling, Charlie, Mr Gunter is sending you a small gift for taking such care of his gem. So we must go to The Look Out, find the pearl and send it back to him and then you can expect to receive his gift. So don't look so unhappy.' He kissed her, smiled into her wondering eyes, and drew her to her feet. 'So why don't we walk up to The Look Out, and find the pearl so that I can take it back to headquarters and arrange for its posting to its rightful owner?'

Charlie sighed, still uncertain how she felt about leaving poor Rosina without the jewel which she had hoped would settle the sad ghost, but understanding all that Ned had said and, of course, agreeing with him.

After luncheon, they walked up the cliff path, watching the sea below, listening to the music of the waves as the tide began to come in, and then found their way through The Look Out gates. The house was empty now and Charlie felt another bout of sadness at its quietness. 'Such a wonderful old place,' she told Ned. 'I do hope somebody will soon come and occupy it again and make it feel happier.'

Ned looked at her intently as they paused by the closed front door. 'We are looking for a home, Charlie, aren't we?' he asked slowly. 'Would you like to live here? Near enough to your old home not to be lonely when I'm at sea, and a real home for us?'

A smile spread over her face and she said softly, 'And for our family—when we have one. Yes, Ned, I should love to live here.' Ideas flashed through her mind. 'And I can continue restoring the grotto and do all I can to help poor Rosina to settle down again.' She looked up into his eyes and put her arms around his neck. 'What a wonderful idea!' she said. 'Can you arrange it before you sail next month?'

Ned nodded, smiling broadly. 'It shall be done, my darling. The Look Out shall be our new home, I promise. And now, let's go to the grotto and find that pearl.'

Charlie's gentle fingers took off the top layer of mortar from the rose sculpture and prised out the pearl. She held it in her hand and they both looked at it, admiring the gleaming polish and the beauty of the round, elegant jewel. 'I'm sure Rosina would have loved to have this in her flower,' said Charlie ruefully, 'but I hope she understands it can't be. Perhaps, when we're living here I can find something else to put in that little hidey-hole to make her happy again.'

'Wait and see,' said Ned, and with the pearl safely in his pocket, led her out of the grotto and once more into the sun. Very slowly, they walked back to Headland House and Charlie heard the music of the ocean, far below the red stone cliff, luring her into saying something quite astonishing. 'Are you sailing off to a country with silvery sandy beaches, everlasting sun and an amazing variety of shells, Ned?' she asked very quietly, stopping as she spoke and catching his hands in hers.

He nodded. 'Probably to the West Indies. Why, Charlie?'

A glow of excitement spread through her. 'Because I want to come with you! You said when we first met that you would like to sail away with me to a far country —well, now we can actually do so! Oh Ned, I know wives can accompany their husbands sometimes, so say yes, please, say yes!'

He said nothing for a few seconds, but she saw his eyes, saw the gleam of joy brighten them and then he took her into his arms. 'Why not, Charlie? Pretend you're my cabin boy, perhaps? Oh yes, we'll go to a sunny land full of music and happy faces. You'll love it, and we'll be together. Of course you can come.'

Laughing, arms around each other, they again started slowly walking back to Headland House. As they entered, and heard the luncheon gong sounding, Charlie whispered to Ned, 'Aunt Jem will have a fit! Especially if I tell her I'm going to wear my breeches, Papa's white shirt and old boots!'

But once they had explained to Papa and his sister that Charlie, Mrs Edmund Drake these days, would be accompanying Captain Drake on his next voyage, before coming home to settle in their new home at The Look Out, Aunt Jem quietened down, blew her nose and then smiled as she said unsteadily, 'What a wonderful idea. And Charlie, on those beaches you will be able to find all the shells you'll ever need. I'm sure the church bazaar organisers will be so pleased!'

The meal ended in plans being made, and then Charlie and Ned took a trip to Mrs Endacott's farm to collect more cream. 'The strawberries need eating up.' Aunt Jem had said, and both Charlie and Ned agreed.

*   *   *

As the remaining days of Ned's leave passed, plans became reality. The Look Out was taken in hand by Charlie's newly engaged domestic staff, cleaned and redecorated and became the home she knew now that she had always wanted. Old, atmospheric, full of past history and comfortable, it lit a wonderful warmth inside her as she went about her new duties.

When one day Ned received a message to say he must report to headquarters, she awaited his return wondering what next might happen. The grotto, these days, was looking less grim and dirty than it had been when first she saw it.

Candles lit up the newly cleaned walls and no more stones littered the floors of the tall chambers and the small, snaking tunnel.

Every day, Charlie looked at Rosina's rose sculpture and tried to think of something that she could offer the little ghost, but no ideas came.

Until Ned returned from his journey and gave her a small package. He smiled, saying, 'It's addressed to you, sweetheart. From Mr Gunter who has now received the pearl you found. And is probably writing to thank you. Open it.'

She did, her fingers trembling a little and wondering what he might say.

His words were few, written in a slanting, uneven sprawl on thick white paper. *To the lady who saved my beautiful pearl from wicked smugglers and jewel thieves. A small gift which I hope she will enjoy during the rest of her blessed life. With many thank yous from your servant, Adolf Gunter.*

She opened the little package around which the letter was fastened and took in a huge breath of amazement. A ring lay there, a gold setting around a pale, rose-coloured shining stone, and quite beautiful.

For a moment Charlie could say nothing. And then she looked into Ned's watchful, loving eyes and whispered, 'It's for Rosina. Of course it is. A ring to go in the centre of her shell flower. Let's go and give it her now . . . a rose stone to finish the sculpture and bring her together with her love.'

Together they went into the grotto, and she put the little ring into its new home, in the centre of the ghost girl's rose sculpture.

Looking at Ned, Charlotte said, 'She'll be happy now,' and they both smiled.

Then went back to their new home to prepare for the next adventure—the voyage to the far land with its abundance of sunshine, and amazing shells, and a new tune of gentle sea music lapping those white, sandy beaches.